Keechie

By Phil Whitley

PublishAmerica
Baltimore

First printing

At the specific preference of the author, PublishAmerica allowed this work to remain exactly as the author intended, verbatim, without editorial input.

ISBN: 1-4137-9587-0
PUBLISHED BY PUBLISHAMERICA, LLLP
www.publishamerica.com
Baltimore

Printed in the United States of America

Keechie

For Martha—
Another Pine
Mtn. Valley Kid
Hear the Drums?

Phil Whitley

First, I want to acknowledge all Native American and First Nations peoples everywhere. My intent was to honor the wonderful cultural heritages and traditions that a paleface can only know from the outside. Any misrepresentation or offense should be considered completely unintentional and without malice, so please accept my apologies in advance as I continue to learn.

A special acknowledgement is also due to all my friends at TPG who were there when the idea for *Keechie* was first formulated. You gave me the motivation to write when I did not feel like a writer, and the courage to continue writing when that feeling seemed to be true.

Part I

Chapter One
First Meeting

"Dat wada give you da shits fer sho. You gots t' bile it furs'," came a voice from no more than six feet away from me.

I nearly jumped over the small spring I was about to drink from. As far as I knew, I was the only soul for miles around. Except for the occasional screech of a blue jay or the skittering of squirrels, there was no other sound.

"What... who... where are you?" I asked as I tried to regain my composure. The voice sounded like a young girl, but had a quality of being older, wiser somehow.

Fern fronds parted slightly to my left, exposing a small brown face with dark walnut eyes—eyes that glinted with humor and intelligence—eyes that hinted of something deeper...

"Whatcher name, boy? Mine's Keechie."

"Uhh, Brian. My name is Brian. You really scared me. Come out so I can see you, okay?"

The face disappeared behind the fern and all was silent again. Just as I was about to call her again, she spoke from behind me.

"So Brine, whatcha doin' out hyer?"

Again, I nearly jumped out of my skin. I was beginning to reply when I turned to face her, but stopped short at the sight. She was tiny—maybe a little over four feet tall—dressed in a simple cotton smock that was obviously homemade. She was barefooted with long, wide-spaced toes that gave the impression of fingers. Her long silky hair was nearly white and held in place by a beaded headband

"I was just exploring. Looking for Indian mounds, arrowheads and stuff," I said. "What are you doing out here?"

"Ah lives hyer. Lived hyer all my life," she said solemnly.

"With your parents?"

"Hee, hee, ain't got none o' dem no mo. Mam died las' yer, and my Pap ain't nevva been 'roun' since I wuz a l'il gurl. Said he wuz a'goin' huntin'. Guess he ain't found nuttin' yet. Hee, hee."

"Since you were a little girl? How old are you now?"

In some ways she seemed older now that I was able to watch her mannerisms and hear her speak more, but you just couldn't tell for sure.

"Well, lessee, Mam said I wuz 'bout fifty when Granny Boo died, an' dat wuz... what... at leas' ten yars ago. We burred her up at da big rock—same place I burred Mam. Right aside 'er. Lotsa us foke burred up dere."

"You're sixty? You look like you're barely a teenager! How did you do it?"

"Furse, by not drankin' pizon wada. Hyer, have somma mine," she said as she passed me a gourdlike thing that was hanging around her neck by a thong. "Hit got some lemon grass and stuff fer flaver."

I took the gourd and tasted. It was good, and cool, and I wiped my mouth as I passed it back to her.

"Thanks, that is good. What were you doing out here?"

"Well, I wuz 'bout to kill me a rabbit when you skeered it away, crashin' through da brush lak you did. Wanna see whar I stays?" she asked as she turned and melted into the forest.

"Is you a'comin'?" she added, sounding like she was already twenty yards ahead of me.

"Wait up. I can't see you!" I pleaded, not knowing why I was about to follow her, except from a great curiosity, and a feeling that I was about to have a real adventure.

I felt no danger from Keechie. After all, I was bigger than she was by far, and a strong sixteen years old. I still couldn't believe she was sixty. In a minute I caught sight of her again and hurried to catch up.

After about fifteen minutes of fighting through brush and vines we came to a small clearing nestled right up against the foot of Pine Mountain. A place I thought I knew like the back of my hand. There were several huge boulders, and between two of them, appeared to be the front half of a shack. A small, sloped roof covered what used to be a porch, but that's all there was of her "house."

"C'mon in, but be shore to wipe yer boots off, hee, hee," she said as she hung her water gourd and knapsack on a hook beneath the porch. "Duck yore head when you gets inside while I lights a cannle. Ain't had no cumpny since Mam passed."

From the pale light of a guttering candle, I could just make out that we were in a cave. Something that I heard was in these mountains, but was never fortunate enough to find. Maybe someone had dug this one, but it looked natural from what little I could make out by the flickering light.

There was a pleasant aroma filling the space—probably from the herbs and bunches of dried roots hanging from every available space above our heads. A rock-lined hearth took up part of the back wall and contained a black iron kettle. Smoke drifted slowly up and disappeared into a crack in the ceiling.

"How big IS this place?" I wondered aloud.

"Don' nobody know fer sho, but my Pap found some opnin's through da rock. Dey be miles an' miles unda da mountin, he tole us—Granny Boo, Mam and me. My baby brother got hisseff lost up in dere sommeres. Pap hunted 'im fer days. Dat wuz when I wuz jus' a l'il girl," she replied almost as if she was thinking aloud to herself.

"Do you ever go to where our houses are, you know… in the valley?" I asked, in an attempt to change the subject.

"Sometime my Pap would take me inta town with 'im. Dat wuz when 'e worked sawmillin' and stuff. He hadda go to da Sto to fetch 'is pay. Dey paid the menfokes at da Sto, hopin' dey buy sumpin' I 'spose… He 'ud get dry beans an' sugar and taters an' baccy an' thangs lak dat. He always got me some canny. I sho did lak canny!" She paused a long moment, seemingly lost in thought.

"He tol' me to not talk to 'em, and especull no Injun talk. 'Don' evva look 'em inna eyes,' he say. 'Dey hates Injuns wuss dan niggers, he say. Nevva did lak dat word, an' I don' even know whut it mean.

"I sho did lak that sto though. Dey had evathang in dere. Shoes dey call brogans, my Pap say, and food in cans. Hee, hee. Furs' time he brought dat can stuff back, my Mam lak to never got into it! He say they was a thang he fergot dat open' dem. Mam beat it open with a rock! Hee, hee."

"Dey had cold meat, food fer cows an' chickens, hammas an' saws an' sich. I sho coulda got spoilt iffen I coulda got mo stuff dere!"

She paused with a wistful look on her face then added, "Afta dat, I juss sometimes goes up t' de top of da mountin and watches da car lights run aroun' da roads down dere. Sometime I can hyer some music a'playin' when da wind's jus' right. Once I sneaked up real close t' one a' dey houses, and could see de fokes inside, movin' aroun'… an' somma dey kids was a'playin' outside. One o' dem spotted me and run inside real fas' lak, a'hollerin' 'Injun, Injun!' So I got 'way from dere inna hurry, I did! Hee, hee."

"Indian? You're an Indian?" I asked, with growing excitement. As far as I knew there hadn't been any Indians around here for over a hundred years!

"Well, my Mam and Granny Boo wuz. My Pap, well, he were blacker'n a crow. He say his mam were Injun though. So I 'spose I more'n haff Injun. Why don'chall lak Injuns?" she added, catching me off-guard.

"Who says we don't like Indians? Why do you think I roam these swampy vine-jungles, looking for Indian stuff? I don't think I've never even SEEN a real Indian! Pictures, yes, and movies on television"

"I read every book I can find on Indians. I study about the Indians that were here, in this part of the country, before the white man killed them or drove them away. I sometimes wish that I WAS an Indian! Don't lump me in with everybody else! ...please?" I blurted, realizing that I was yelling pretty loud. "Sorry, I got carried away."

"Dat's okay. Dey din' drive us ALL away. Hee, hee... ner kilt us all neither. Granny Boo's granny an' her family 'fused to leave hyer when da sojers come an' tol' 'em dey gots t' leave. Dey came hyer to this cave an' hid, an' no one ever foun' 'em. Din' even know to look fer 'em, my Pap say. He say dat Injuns could juss disappear inta da fores'. Slip away lak shadders, he say. I ken do it too! Hee, hee." We been hyer ever since!"

I couldn't believe it! An honest-to-god Indian still living here! I remembered something I had in my pocket that I had found earlier today close to the spring.

"Look at this," I said as I offered it to her.

It was a perfect chert arrowhead about two inches long. She took it and looked at it closely. She raised it over her head with her lips moving silently.

"Juss honerin' m' ancestors" she said as she looked at it closely.

"Hit ain't from 'roun' hyer. Looks lak somma dat my Granny Boo's fambly traded fer. Plains people she call 'em, you know, da ones from da souf'... I still gots a chunk o' hit hyer 'roun' hyer somwhars. I tries to save it when I kin. Ain't no mo a 'comin'." she said as she handed it back to me.

"I know," I answered, realizing my chance to show off my Indian knowledge. "Chert is fairly common in middle Georgia, around Butler and Reynolds, but not around here. I once found an almost perfect bird point down there!"

"Yep, Dey traded 'em pelts fer dat stuff. Beaver, deer, rabbit, whuteva dey had fer it. Hit make a good sharp knife, hit does!"

She hesitated and looked me in the eyes.

"Kin I trus' you, Brine?"

"Trust me? Why would you ask that?" I felt kinda hurt at the question.

"You be da onliest one know 'bout me hyer. I felt de call t' talk to you today. Seemed 'portant, but I wants t' stay private lak, ya unnerstan'?" she asked, still looking deeply in my eyes.

"You can trust me," I promised, with a goose-bumpy feeling that something very important was taking place.

"But it's getting late and I need to get home before dark. My folks will be worried." I began moving towards the porch reluctantly. I was afraid that if I left now I may never see her again.

"Can I come back sometimes?"

"Sho you kin, Brine. I wants you to, an' I wantcha t' have dis."

Keechie took a small leather bag from around her neck and placed in over my head.

"Don' evva take it off, er you has bad luck or sompin'. Hit were Granny Boo's. I come wit'cha partway, 'cuz we needs t' talk some mo. I shows you da easy way dis time. Hee, hee."

Chapter Two
Medicine Bag

It was almost dark when I got home, and my mother was in the driveway just about to blow the car horn in our agreed-on signal that meant, "You better be home before your dad gets here!"

"I was getting worried about you. Supper's almost done, so get inside and wash up... and take off those boots!" She had stopped asking me where I'd been or what I'd been up to lately. I always showed her my "finds" if there were any, and sometimes I had a dead rabbit or squirrel with me. She wouldn't take part in the skinning and cleaning process, but she would cook them for me. She preferred her meat out of the display cases at my dad's store.

"I found a really neat arrowhead today, Mom," I said as I handed it to her, remembering to hide the little bag that Keechie had hung around my neck as we parted. It was made of rabbit pelt that had been tanned and chewed soft. It contained several small stones, a bear claw, dried herbs, corn pollen, the tip of a deer's antler and some of Granny Boo's Power Bundle,' Keechie had told me.

She gave it a quick look and handed it back to me.

"I wonder how long it has been lying there, just waiting for you to pick it up. The Indians were gone from here long before your granddaddy ever came here and settled. He said there was nothing here but forests when he arrived, and that was in 1932. He never saw any Indians."

My dad got home about thirty minutes after me, and we had supper. Afterwards, I showed him my new arrowhead and got out my collection to add it to. I labeled it carefully, noting the date and location where I found it.

"It's not from around here, Dad. It looks like the chert one I found in Butler. Wonder how it got here?"

"Good strong bow... maybe they SHOT it here! How do I know?" My dad wasn't much on Indian lore.

"Over a hundred miles... aww, Dad! Reckon they traded for it? You know, like animal hides or something?"

"Probably. They didn't carry much money around in those days, I don't reckon." Sometimes he did have a really sharp sense of humor.

After a couple hours of television, I got ready for bed. Tomorrow was Saturday and I planned on a full day with Keechie. She was going to show me the burial ground of her people. I had a hunch that I already knew where "the big rock" was.

If I was right, it was already one of my favorite spots on the mountain. I called it my "Power Place." I had never been there from the valley, but had always hiked up the road from my house to the highway that ran the crest of the mountain. There was a trail there that led to the rock. It was a large outcropping of granite near the highest point on the mountain. There was nothing all that special about it, except for the "feel" of the place. Kinda like that feeling you get walking into a church. But I had never seen any graves there, and I had explored all around it many times.

I lay there in bed with the lights off, listening to the night sounds–the lonesome call of a whippoorwill, the screech of an owl, and the inevitable bullfrogs, and thought about the day I had just had. It almost didn't seem real, but the small pouch around my neck was proof that it really had happened. I reached up and touched it, thinking about Keechie and the conversation we had after I left her cave, then drifted off to sleep.

An old woman stood on the big rock at the top of the mountain. Her arms were outstretched towards the sky and she was singing. The words were not recognizable but I knew what they meant. Her voice, although soft, were heard through all living things. She was calling the animals to her valley. She was asking for them to give their lives for her tribe for food. She promised them honor and gratitude. She was asking the fish to fill the streams and rivers, the deer to provide clothing from their hides and their flesh for nourishment, and the beaver and mink for their hides for trade. The Song was irresistible, and I sensed the animals responding in great numbers. She called them Brothers and Sisters...

The smell of bacon frying and coffee brewing woke me. Dad was getting ready for work and Mom was cooking breakfast.

"I'm going up to the rock today and maybe fish the creek," I said as nonchalantly as I could.

I always had my hunting bag ready, and I was more excited than I wanted to show. I had an extra skinning knife that I planned on giving to Keechie as a gift. I had noticed that she still used flint for cutting, and I thought she would appreciate a real knife.

Dad gave me the usual, "Watch out for snakes," warning, and Mom told me to listen out for "The Horn" in case she needed me.

Soon I was off, following the creek upstream through the woods as I had done yesterday, up to where it became several smaller streams, then turned due west, toward the mountain.

Keechie was there at the spring just as yesterday. She was skinning a rabbit and didn't seem at all surprised at my arrival.

"I heared you a'comin' a mile off," she said as she wiped her stone blade off on the grass.

"Well, you need to teach me to walk like an Indian, then," I replied, disappointed because I was really trying to be quiet.

"Ya gots to BE an Injun to walk lak one," she quipped back, with a twinkle in her dark eyes.

"But I kin teach ya to walk mo quietlike!"

I noticed the hide she had just removed from the rabbit. She had washed it off in the spring and laid it inside-out in the sun to dry. It was almost perfect, with only the belly slit where she had dressed it out.

"Teach me to skin a rabbit like that?"

Since we didn't save the pelts, my dad had taught me to start from the back, which ruined the hide.

"Sho, I teach ya! Whut ya cut wit?" she asked me.

That reminded me of my gift I had for her. I opened my pack and pulled out the Case XX Skinner in its original sheath.

"One just like this. But this one is yours," I said as I handed it to her.

She looked almost reverent as she slowly took it. She felt the leather sheath and examined the brads that held it together. She took the leather thongs that were on the bottom for leg strapping and tasted it!

"Cow hide." she said appreciatively.

Then she fiddled with the snap that secured the knife in place until it snapped open. She went to her knees and slowly drew the blade out. Her eyes were glistening as she lifted it up towards the sky with both hands, as if it were an offering. Then she took it in her right hand and sliced her left palm open!

"Knife ain't really yores 'til hit tastes yore blood, my Granny Boo say. An' I gots to pay ya fo it. Knife gift cut friendship. Hyer, I brung dis fo ya anyhows," and handed me a perfect flint spear point almost six inches long.

"Dat wuz my Granny Boo's husbin's. He was the son o' de las' Mico... chief... of our clan befo' dey went west. He made it hisseff."

We were both speechless for a long moment as we both studied our new treasures. I looked across at her and opened my arms for a hug. She gave me a serious look, then took my shoulders and looked me in the eyes,

"Yo a good boy, Brine. De Spirits done tole me dat furs' time I see ya—an' dat wuz a while back! Ya cares 'bout things—animals, an' plants an' Injun stuff. Didja evva dream about Injun stuff, Brine?"

She was trying to sound spontaneous, but I could tell it was important to her —like she had been waiting for the right moment to ask, and that she already knew the answer.

"Well, yes, but nothing like the dream I had last night. It was so real... like it wasn't a dream at all."

I told her about the old woman standing on the bluff, calling the animals, and the beautiful song she was singing.

"Did it soun' lak dis?" she asked me. Then she closed her eyes, leaned her head back, and sang the same song I had heard. The words were still unrecognizable, but I KNEW it was the song. The feeling was there same as in the dream.

"Dat's da 'Come to Me' Song. My Granny Boo taught it to me. Only works wit ever otha girl-child. My Mam could sang it, but hit din' work fer 'er. Only da grandchiles could make it work. Same as the Healin' stuff. My Mam could make da potions iffen Granny Boo tol' 'er whut t' put in. But she din't know herseff wut to put in, but I does! Hee, hee."

"How does it work, Keechie?" I asked her when I could speak again.

"Well, you see, hit seem dat evathang is juss part of evathang else. Rocks, trees, sky, dirt, animals, and peoples. The song jus' reminds all dose thangs dat dey is a part a' hit all, and dey's got dey own job t'do. We be pre-shatin' hit, and we gots to let 'em know dat too. Evathang gonna come back aroun' 'ventual lak. Big ol' wheel be a'turnin'. Sometime you's at de top, but den you gots to take yore turn at de bottom, knowin' dat de Wheel gonna brang ya right back up on top soon 'nuff."

Somehow the wisdom of those words struck home to me as if I had heard them before. She was talking about something more than the food chain, but it was related. This was more of a spiritual thing than the physical need for food.

After a moment she said, "Now let's us get back to da cave. I gots ta get dis hyer rabbit a'biling. Already got de udda stuff in da pot.

When we gets back dis affanoon we goin' t' have us a fine stew! An', I gets to try out m' new knife!"

Back at her "home", she deftly cut the rabbit up into smaller pieces and dropped them into the already wonderful smelling mixture in the pot.

"What all's in there?" I asked.

"Ohhh, corn, beans, sage, some squash, unyens, de las' of de salt my Pap brung, some taters and mushrooms I fount. Oughtta be real tasty," she answered.

"Ready to see the burrin' ground?"

"Yep!" I said, wondering if I should tell her that I thought already knew where it was.

The trail looked like it had been made by animals, occasionally disappearing into the brush. Loose rock made it difficult walking at times, but it wasn't all that steep. This end of the Appalachians wasn't all that high, and there was no actual climbing required. After an hour, I could see the crest ridge.

A car could be heard travelling along what we called the "Scenic Highway", which ran along the top of the mountain from the valley all the way to Warm Springs, about twenty-five miles away.

It was my rock. I knew it before we could see it, for I had explored the area many times, only from the top down. I never knew where the trail was from below. There was the same feel of being in a holy place that I knew so well. Keechie told me to remove my boots before we got there.

"Dis be sacred ground," she said.

"Many of my people be hyer. We needs t' touch da ground so dey knows it be us. Ought'n even be hyer, lessen you needs to." She began softly chanting under her breath.

I didn't see anything that looked like graves, and was wondering how a grave could even be dug, with all the rock around. Surely it extended beneath the ground as well. The "Rock" was only an outcrop, and I knew there was a whole lot more beneath out feet. She pointed to a space between two large boulders.

"Granny Boo's dere. An' over dere, nex' to dat big boulder is her grandfather's father, da big Mico... dat means da Chief. His Injun name mean 'Bull Killer', cuz da deed dat earn him 'is name, 'most coss 'im 'is life! Not only from da bull, but from da white man who owned it! Hee, hee. Kilt it wid a spear, 'e did. He were jus' a boy, on his Spirit Quest. One throw! Granny Boo tol' us dey all ate real good DAT month! Hee, hee!"

So the burials were in between the rocks. Not in the ground as I was expecting. But some of the spaces didn't seem large enough to fit a body into. I asked her about that.

Well, dey usta bury da dead in da valley, in da swampy groun'. 'Roun' two yars later dey dig 'em up. Juss bones leff, doncha know? Den dey put 'em in jars, or juss blankets and put 'em in da honor places up hyer. Dey's hunnerts of 'em 'roun' hyer! Da real old 'uns would keep dey skull in da house, watchin' ova da fambly."

I had heard about that custom in other countries, but I didn't realize that it was practiced by the Native Americans around here.

"They kept the skulls of their relatives in their homes?"

"Summa dem did, but we din't do dat later on. We leff 'em all togedder. Dey usta put dey stuff inna grave wit' 'em too, but dat made some o' da bad 'uns wanna dig 'em up to git it. We always juss put one or two l'il thangs dat wuz speshull to 'em in dere wit' 'em. Nuttin' nobody else would want."

She paused, looking at me intently, seemingly considering her words carefully.

"De speshull stuff we keeps at home to 'member 'em by. 'Sides, dey spirit come to visit dey stuff, an' gets to see us too! Hee, hee! I shows you some o' hit later."

"I already knew this place, Keechie. But from the top. I come here a lot, just to think and feel the Power."

"Hee, hee, Brine! 'Member I tol' ya that I had seed you a lot? Furs' time I seed ya, you wuz up dere on de rock, justa sittin' anna rockin' back an' forth. Thass when I knowed you wuz da one white person I could trust! Dat stuff don' know no color er race ner nuttin'. Dat be a heart thang. Been watchin' you evva since!"

I watched Keechie as she made her rounds of the burial ground, apparently talking to her ancestors. She had dressed in more traditional style than she had the day before. The cotton dress she wore today was more "Indian" in appearance, with beads and porcupine quills worked into patterns. Her hair was in a long braid down her back, and had a beaded rawhide clasp at the top and bottom.

I opened my pack and dug for the beef jerky I had stashed. She joined me under a lightning-struck oak tree, and I offered her a strip.

"Make dis yerseff?" she asked, as she bit into the tough meat.

"Nope, I bought this already made. I have made it, though. I'll bet you could make better!"

"Hee, hee… mebbe not as spicy, but I sho has made my share of hit. Times wuz, we practicly lived offen it fer da whole winter!"

It was early afternoon when we started back down the mountain. I picked her memory of the things Granny Boo had told her about her tribe before she was born.

"Well, dey lived in cabins mostly. Da village was called a 'talofa', Granny Boo say. Our tribe is Osochi. Came hyer from across da `Hoochie River, over in Alabamer. Granny Boo say we gots kinfoke out west – ones dat leff hyer when her mam wuz juss born. `Er Granny n' grampa stayed hyer, but `er Granny's older sister, Cornsilk, n' `er husbin leff. She were pregnernt when she leff. Granny Boo say Cornsilk wuz de mos' powful medison woman she evva heerd `bout."

As we made our way down the trail, she would occasionally stop and show me a plant or shrub.

"Dat 'un be good fer fever, and dat 'un good fer cleanin' out yer biles," she informed me.

I recognized some of them, and told her what I knew about them.

"That willow bark is good for headaches. Same stuff in it as aspirin," I tried out on her.

She flashed a smile at me and added, "Yep, but ya gots t' get to da green bark inside. Dat's wher da good be. "Know whut dis is?" she asked, pointing to a small plant.

"Sassafras! Got to dig the roots, though. My mom makes tea from it!"

"Yep. We calls it yeller root. Good stuff, but hit don't keep good. Gots t' get it fresh fer it to work good. Clean yer blood."

She seemed rather proud of me for my limited knowledge, but it was something I had been drawn to since I was a little kid. My grandmother had acquired a lot of what she called "Injun medicine", and I had learned a lot from her.

"You never know when you may need a "cure" and there's no drugstore handy," she told me over and over. "Besides, sometimes that store bought cure is worse than the ailment!"

Chapter Three
Keechie's Cave

As we approached her dwelling from above, I made it a point to smell for any trace of smoke from her hearth. Nothing. And as we approached the cave itself, I was curious as to how visible it was from that perspective. It was not until we were in the clearing itself that you could see the old ramshackle porch that hid the entrance, but still I wondered how hunters had not found her place in all these years.

We removed our footwear on the porch and went inside. Now you could smell the aroma of that rabbit stew, and it smelled GOOD! Keechie unrolled a mat in front of the hearth and told me to sit. She moved out of my line of vision, and when I turned, she was gone! The door covering had not opened, for I would have seen the light from outside.

Just as I was about to call her, a blanket on the wall to my right moved, and there she was... bowls in hand.

"Only gets out da good stuff fer speshul compny," she said. She rinsed the bowls from a pot of water near the hearth and threw the remainder out the "door."

As she filled the first bowl and handed it to me, she said, "Hopes ya lak it, ain't nuff salt fer me!"

She filled her a bowl and sat across from me. The spoons were wooden, greatly aged and smooth from use.

"You said you just used the last of the salt that your father had brought, and that was a long time ago. Just how much salt did he bring to begin with?" I asked her. It seemed that after almost sixty years a lot of salt would have been used.

"Big ol' block he brung. Hard to carry too. Hit had a hole inna center dat we used t' stick a pole through, t' make carrin' it easier."

I immediately knew what he had brought. A fifty pound block of salt with a hole in it could have only been one thing. My dad sold them in his store. It was a "salt lick" for cattle.

"Was it white or brown, Keechie?"

"White. Pyo salt, hit was. Good stuff too. Hate to see it go."

White. Then it was pure salt. The brown salt licks also contained other minerals that were especially for cows and horses. I made a mental note to add salt to the things I wanted to bring her on my next trip. A big box of Kosher Salt was just the ticket!

The stew was the most delicious I had ever tasted. Maybe it was thinking of the source, but taste buds were hard to fool, besides rabbit was not my favorite wild game. It was okay, but venison was my favorite.

I neared the bottom of my bowl and paused to see how Keechie handled the last of the liquid. Thank goodness, she turned the bowl up and drank directly from it. I did the same.

"Mo?" she asked with a full ladle at the ready.

"Yes, please. This it so good, Keechie! You could open up a restaurant!"

"I could... whut? Whut's a... restrunt?"

"Sorry, it's a place where they sell food already prepared. It's for people who don't have time to cook or make it themselves."

"Dey better be a'brangin' dey own rabbits, den," she said, with a hint of the humor I came to expect from her.

When I finished my second bowl, she took them both and rinsed them out again with great care.

"Dese wuz Granny Boo's bowls. She made 'em herseff. Put da designs on 'em an' all. Dey sho be spechul t' me."

They were beautiful, simple as they were, and I said so.

"She were good wit' thangs lak dat," she said, and turned to put them away.

This time I watched where she went. Behind the blanket on the wall was an opening, almost as wide as the blanket, but in an oval shape.

"May I see in there, Keechie?" I asked.

"Sho you kin. C'mon in. Hit's whar I keeps mos' everthang. Kinda da sto room," she answered as she opened the blanket for me.

Several candles were already burning and I was speechless. It looked like something from a museum of Indian history. Masks, headdresses, spears and beautifully quilled blankets covered the walls. Hides of all sorts were draped and piled over everything at floor level. Racks of beads, belts and necklaces were hanging from pegs on every wall.

The room was easily twelve feet wide, and at least that long.

She placed the bowls into a chest beside the opening and said, "All's I got leff of my whole tribe. Somma dis stuff goes back, oh, a coupla hunnert years, I spose. Mos' a' it came from Granny Boo's clan. Dey uz da chiefs."

I had never seen a real spear with everything still attached. The one I was staring at was simply awesome. It was at least eight feet long and perfectly straight. The point was probably a foot long and was obviously obsidian. Black volcanic glass from only the Rockies, as I recalled. Some of the sharpest known cutting surgical instruments were made of obsidian, even with stainless steel as a contender. The shaft was elaborately carved, and decorated with eagle feathers.

"Dat were Granny Boo's Grampa's daddy's spear. 'Member old Bull Killer I tolt you 'bout? Dat wuz his spear. He wuz a'holdin' it when he died right up dere on dat rock we wuz at t'day. He dressed hisseff up in all 'is chief stuff an' went up dere, an' when da sojers come an' tol' 'em dey hadda go. Granny Boo say dey tol' her dat he was stannin' dere a'prayin' to da Father Spirit. He say, 'Do whut ya gots ta do, but I stays hyer where my people is burred.' Right den, he juss fell over. Guess dat were 'is answer. He still hyer. I showed him to you today, 'member?"

"Yes, I remember, Keechie. Bull Killer must be very proud of you for staying here just like he did. I just know it!"

I could barely speak, and the novelty of all these artifacts took on a deeper, more spiritual meaning than just their museum value. These things were the soul, the memories – the very heart of a people. A people who never felt they owned the land, but considered it on loan from the Great Spirit. They made few ripples on the Pond of Life, and were exterminated for their innocence. I was overcome with emotion and went to my knees, feeling the beginning of tears in my eyes.

Keechie pulled me to my feet, a few tears of her own showing, and wiped my face with her hands.

"Here, young chief Brine. Hol' it. Hit's got a feel to it dat hep ya unnerstan'."

She had taken the spear from the wall and was offering it to me.

I took it, expecting some ancient Indian curse to strike me down, but it felt warm and accepting, as if Bull Killer himself had offered it to me. Energy flowed from it in almost visible waves. I could hear drums pounding in my head, as if there was a ceremony of great importance taking place in a dimension just outside this one.

An image appeared in my mind of a man apparently wearing a leopard mask. He was smiling at me as only a cat can smile.

Keechie spoke in a husky whisper, "Didja hyer da drums, Brine? As long as dey's someone who kin hyer da drums, da People will nevva die."

"I heard them, Keechie. And there seemed to be a cat man smiling at me. Do you suppose that was the chief?"

She looked surprised, and appeared to be about to speak, but then took the spear from my hands and placed it back on the wall.

We walked around the room slowly as she told me what she knew of the relics.

"Dat blanket wuz made by Granny Boo fer 'er weddin'. Hit show da comin' togedder of da Puma Clan and da Wind Clan. Granny Boo wuz Kowakuce, da Puma Clan. Dis Medicine Bag wus her father's. He wuz war chief o' da Nokuse, dat mean de Bear Clan. Dey be powful medicine in dat 'un!"

As we were leaving the room, something I had noticed before, but had not registered until now, caught my attention. The flame from each candle was pointing toward the back wall. Air was flowing in that direction, so that must be where the opening was to the deeper recesses of the cave!

"Is there another passageway here, Keechie?" I knew I was eventually going to HAVE to explore this cave. I had searched for years to find one, had read every book I could find on spelunking, and had visited some of the ones in Tennessee that were open to the public. This was just to great a chance to pass up.

"Dey be opnin's all over da place, Brine. Somma dem don' go nowheres, er dey juss gets too small fer a person t' fit. Somma dem open up t' mo big rooms lak dis 'un. But don' be a'thinkin' 'bout goin' off in dere. Done lost me one brother in dere. Mam never did get over dat 'un. Den hit were juss about a yer later when Pap leff us. He tried dat whole yer t' fine 'im. Den he jus leff."

I quickly changed the subject so she wouldn't see how excited I was about exploring the cave.

"Where was your Daddy from, Keechie?"

"He from Luz-Anna. Run away from dere too. Almost kilt a man with a 'shetty-knife, he say. He work in da cane field dere. We usta grow somma dat here, we did. Granny Boo made sirp out a' it. Sho wuz good!"

"Pap wuz near dead when Mam foun' 'im up onna ridge aside da road up on top. She wuz up at da wemmin's cabin, havin' 'er firs' moon-time. Hee, hee. She brung 'im dere and nuss 'im back to life. Dey hat me 'roun two year later."

"Granny Boo din' lak 'im at furs', but she took to 'im well 'nuff later on. He were a hart worker and brung us stuff from da sto. Hadda have money t' get dat stuff! Hee, hee. He say he wuz name afta Gawg Washton. Say dat he wuz da fuss Big Chief o' da white man's lan', Merka. Pap try ta teach me lotta stuff lak dat afore he leff."

It was getting late when we went back outside, so I started getting my stuff together.

"Oh, Keechie, here's a special stone to sharpen your knife with," I said as I handed her a six inch carborundum stone.

"I'll show you how to use it." I took my own knife out of its sheath and demonstrated.

She tried it on her own knife and thanked me.

Once again she walked partway with me, and once again, gave me a friendly pat on the shoulder.

Chapter Four
Gifts for Keechie

There were only two weeks left before school started. I had worked at my dad's store all summer and he always gave me the last three weeks off before school—my "vacation", as it were. It would be my sophomore year at Harris County High. I had just bought my first car—a 1952 Chevrolet two-door coupe. Paid three hundred dollars for that baby, only to then realize that you also have to have insurance, tires, and all the other hidden costs of owning an automobile.

My funds were pretty low, but I had some things I needed. All the stores were closed on Sunday, so I spent the day after church going over and over my supplies, making a list of the additional stuff I was going to get.

I was going to explore that cave. I knew in my heart that no matter what obstacles came in my path—my own fear included—was going to stop me.

Monday morning I was on my way to Chipley, where I could shop without having to answer too many questions. I first went to the Ace Hardware and got two kerosene lamps, a gallon of kerosene, a small funnel and a box of a dozen candles for Keechie.

Then for my own use, I added a couple tubes of electrician's pull string (500 feet per tube), extra batteries for my flashlights, and a pair of cotton work gloves. I had everything else I needed—at least I hoped so.

Next I went to the grocery store and bought black pepper and other spices, two boxes of kosher salt and five pounds of salt pork (streak-o-lean). I added a peck of corn meal, five pounds of dried beans and two very nice sirloin steaks. I was going to grill them for Keechie and I this afternoon. In my camping stuff was a small cast iron grill top that I planned to give her for her fireplace.

I drove up to the top of the mountain and pulled into the almost hidden trail that led to the "Rock" that had become so familiar to me over the years. But now I saw it in a new light—as that of the burial place of many of the local Creek Indians. Several of them had been killed by white men for no reason except that of being an Indian.

I took my new purchases down to the foot of the outcropping, along with the bag of gear I already had accumulated and stashed them —except for the salt and the meat. That was to be a special treat for Keechie when I made my appearance later.

Driving home slowly, I tried to think of anything I had forgotten, and how I was going to to convince Keechie that I would be okay in exploring her cave. My folks already knew I was "going camping" for a couple of days, so I was as ready as I was ever going to be.

When I got home, I packed up the salt, the steaks and my sleeping roll and told Mom good-bye. I then headed up the creek towards Keechie's cave.

Keechie wasn't at the spring when I passed it. The cave was silent and deserted. I sat down on a boulder outside and waited for almost an hour until she came walking up, carrying a large basket of corn.

"Yore gettin' purdy good at Injun walkin', Brine. I din' hyer ya comin' dat time!" she joked as she dropped the basket of corn down. "I hadda git da last o' da corn in befo' winner set in. Dis be my third trip! I got serval patches 'round hyer. Dis wuz da last."

"Well, a couple of those ears ought to go pretty good with this," I told her as I pulled out the two thick steaks.

"Woo-wee," she exclaimed as she took them. "Whut IS dis? Wait, don' tell me... smells lak somepin' I smelt befo'... Hit's cow meat! I ain't had dat since I wus a little 'un! I thank I could eat it raw, juss lak it is!" she said with obvious glee.

"And here, while I'm thinking about it..." and handed her the two boxes of salt.

"Whut dis?" She said as she studied the boxes. I had already assumed that she probably couldn't read, and I watched as she smelled, then shook the box.

"Hit don' got no smell, but hit's heavy..."

I opened the little spout on the side and shook some of the grains into her hand.

"Taste it, Keechie."

She looked at me intensely, then stuck her tongue to her palm.

"Hit's SALT! she squealed. "Hit be real salt! I wuz a'wondrin' whut I wuz a'gonna do widdout salt! Thankee, Brine. You done sho made dis woman ver' happy!"

"Well, you did share the last you had with me. Let's put this away for now, Keechie. I've got some more stuff up at the rock I've got to get down here before it gets dark. I brought it up there earlier today – in my car."

"You got a ca', Brine? she asked. "I din' know you hadda ca'."

"Yep. Just got it this summer. You don't have a road to here, or I would have drove here and took you for a ride."

"Ain't never rid in a ca' befo', but me and Pap once rid inna back of a truck from town. Old man brung us right up to da bridge down dere close to whar you lives. Hit were faster'n a deer could run! Da wind wuz so strong I could'n talk. I wuz a'skeered, but Pap hel' onta me real tight and tol' me t' watch da sky. Hit din' move so fas'. Whut else you done brung? Less go git it now. I put dis meat an' salt in da cave."

She was like a kid at Christmas, so excited over such small things. I almost had to run to keep up with her to the rock. When we got there, she could hardly wait to see the rest of the things I had brought. The lamps got the most attention. She didn't even know what they were, but the glass bases and the globes were amazing to her. She had never seen glass except in the form of bottles and windowpanes in town, and these were beautiful to her. I explained them to her, then showed her the kerosene fuel that burned on the wicks to make light.

I stressed to her how dangerous the fuel could be, and how she should always keep it closed and away from fire. I put a small amount into one of the lamps and lit it, showing her how to "trim the wick" for the best flame with no smoke. In our day of electric lights, it was humbling to watch someone see a kerosene lamp for the first time.

She was estatic. Then I showed her the rest of the supplies. The cornmeal was something she was familiar with, having ground her own corn. The candles were familiar too, but very appreciated. The black pepper was a complete unknown to her.

She smelled it and immediately sneezed.

"Dis be medison?"

"No, well, to some it is… as are all these spices, but you can flavor food with them too," I explained.

"You'll figure them out. You're a great cook."

The dried beans were no mystery to her, since she dried her own, but I figured they would help her get through the winter.

"Now let's get this stuff back to the cave. I can stay a couple of days… if you'll have me?" I asked.

"Sho you kin stay, Brine. I ain't had no one atall stay wit' me since Mam died. I be glad o' da compny!"

It was almost dark by the time we reached the cave. We put away the supplies and I filled both lamps. They made the room warm with their light and Keechie once again studied them intensely.

"Dey makes da place come alive, Brine. I cain't thank you 'nuff. I kin see lak hit wuz day in hyer!"

We arranged a few stones in her fireplace and placed the cast iron grill on them. Soon the steaks were sizzling and the corn was roasting over the bed of coals. We talked while they cooked. I had rubbed the steaks with salt and pepper while she started a pot of dried bean with squash and onions. While we waited for the meal to be ready, we talked—just small talk like friends do.

Luckily, I had remembered she only had bowls, and had added two of my mom's old melanine plates to my pack. Can't eat a steak out of a bowl, was my thinking.

When the steaks were medium rare, I put them onto the plates. We both used our hunting knives and had a royal feast, sitting cross-legged across from each other. No forks needed!

The corn, although hot, we ate out of hand. It had a flavor that was unique to any I had ever tasted. It had a more "corn" taste and was very sweet, but I attributed it to the special evening we were having.

It was a treat for me to watch Keechie savor the meat. She was so childlike in her approach to everything, and this night was very special to both of us. We had bonded on some level that was outside of age differences, racial differences or technological advances. We were simply two humans who admired and respected the other for things that were on a much higher plane.

She rinsed the plates and brought them to me.

"They're yours to keep. You may find a use for them later."

"Did yore Mam make dese, Brine?" she asked as she examined them closely.

"No, they were bought in a set of what we call "china" many years ago. My mom has all new ones now. They are not expensive. I can bring you more if you want."

"Well, dey's spechul to me. I ain't never seed plates lak dese befo'. I put 'em up real safe."

We put out one of the lamps and sat in front of the fire for several hours just talking about life in general. Keechie fascinated me with her vast knowledge about nature and its gifts. Many things that we take for granted were her daily reminders of a "Great Spirit" who provided everything a person needed to survive. She always remembered to give thanks for these gifts—something that modern man forgets to do in his eternal quest for a better life, or a better job, or a better house or even a faster car.

Keechie rolled out some hide blankets for us to make our beds upon, then banked the coals in the hearth.

"Make it easier to start da fire in da mawnin'," she explained.

"I sleep closes' t' da door. I gets up a lot durin' da night. Da night be my favrite time—I laks to lissen t' da night sounds, and watch da moon an' stars. Most ever night I sees some red an' white flashin' lights cross da sky. Wunner if dey be a sign…"

"Probably just airplanes," I said, realizing that maybe she hadn't connected the planes flying over in the daytime with the lights at night. Frequently they were so high there was no sound.

"My Pap told me airplanes had a hunnert people 'er mo' in 'em. I couldn't get my mind 'roun' DAT! Dey looks so small! He tried to 'splain how dey stay up dere, but he din' quite unnerstan' hisself. He juss say dat's how rich people travel."

"I'll show you one day, Keechie. It isn't magic. It's just technology."

"Hee, hee. Dat be magic if I could juss SAY dat word, Brine! Let 'lone unnerstan' it."

I rolled out my sleeping bag onto the pile of blankets and placed my pack at the head to use as a pillow. Keechie disappeared into the other room for several minutes and returned with a clay pot and a gourd dipper.

"Hyer's some fresh wada iffen you gets thirsty durin' da night. I likes my wada in da night. Prolly why I gets up so much. Hee, hee."

I started to take out my little transistor radio, but thought better of it. It seemed too out of place for this cave and for this journey back in time. I decided that I would show it to her later.

We settled in for the night and I was soon asleep, thinking about how I was going to tell Keechie about my plans to explore the cave.

Chapter Five
Inside the Mountain

I had awakened several times during the night and could hear Keechie's breathing. Once I woke just as she was coming back through the door. I filled a gourd of water and drank it.

"Everthang's alright, Brine. Juss da night critters doin' whut dey do."

"Wasn't worried a bit, Keechie. I sleep outside a lot. The four-legged critters don't scare me. It's the ones with two legs that you got to worry about. "

"Hee, hee, don' I know dat! But dose kind don' come 'roun' hyer much."

Morning came soon after. Keechie woke me raking the coals around and placing fresh wood on them. Soon a fire was blazing.

"Want me to fix us something to eat? I have been known to cook up a pretty good breakfast!"

She smiled at me in an almost dare.

I took a small iron frying pan out of my pack, then set about slicing off some thin strips of the salt pork I had brought. I rinsed off most of the salt and started it sizzling in the pan. Next I put on a pot of water to boil. Grits were another staple in my camping pack, and after the water was boiling briskly I added the grits and a pinch of salt. I liked mine with pepper but I waited for that. Keechie hadn't commented about the pepper yet and she could add it or not.

She was duly impressed. We ate everything and could have eaten more.

"Dat poke shore would do good in a pot o' beans!" she said.

"I'se had grits befo' when Pap wuz still hyer. He say hit come from corn."

"Yep, Keechie. My folks call it 'boiling meat' and put it in most of their beans, peas and greens when they cook them. I've also seen some pokeweed near here. You ever cook that?"

What it look lak, Brine? Prolly did. If hit can be et, I prolly done et it!"

'Well, when it gets older, it has these purple berries on a kind of stalk. Big leaves. The main stem is kind of hollow. Some say the berries are poisonous, but the birds eat them."

"I knows just da one! De roots be medison, but you gots to be ver', ver' keerful wit' 'em. Yep, I eats da leaves when dey's young. Old 'uns be too tough. I mixes 'em wit' otha leaves 'cause dey be purdy strong!"

We talked some more about wild foods, and then I dropped the bombshell.

"Keechie, I want to explore the cave some more. I brought some stuff that will make it safer for me. Would you mind?"

"I already figgered you wanna do dat. I seed it in yo eyes. I juss don' wanna lose nobody else up in dere," she said sadly.

"Would you show me the way to get started?" I asked her, not expecting the answer she gave.

I started pulling out the equipment I had brought, and showed her the twine I was going to use to mark my trail so I could always find my way back, and then the flashlights and extra batteries.

She gave a long sigh and took me into the other room. She parted a curtain of deerhide and led me through.

"Dis be whar I gets my wada."

It was a beautiful little pool of water, lined with rock that someone had added. The water flowed down from about three feet above the surface of the pool from a crack higher up in the wall. To the right of the crack and slightly higher up was another small opening. It would be a belly crawl but not too difficult.

"Juss past dis opnin', dey be another big room. On the back wall o' dat one be anotha opnin', a little bigger'n dis 'un. Dat's whar Pap thought my brother went. Nobody 'cept my Pap evva been furder dan dat."

"I won't stay long the first time, Keechie. Don't worry. I'll be real careful... I promise."

I quickly gathered my pack and tied the twine around a boulder. It would unwind as I made my way into the deeper recesses of the cave.

I gave her a smile and a pat on the shoulder and started out.

This first passage wasn't difficult. It was large enough to make my way on my hand and knees, but I only went about twenty feet before coming to the large room Keechie had told me about.

Shining my light around showed no evidence of human occupation. The ceiling was about fifteen feet high, and on the back wall I could see the opening Keechie had mentioned. I made my way to it, and once again crawled through on my hands and knees. This passage was much smaller, but I still didn't feel too confined.

After about thirty feet, traveling slightly upward, I came to another opening. This room was smaller than the first two, but still large enough for me to stand. I took a drink from my canteen and waited for my breathing to subside. I was now beyond the directions Keechie had given me.

Looking around the room I saw no openings at first. But to my right I noticed a pile of rocks that somehow looked out of place, as if they had been intentionally stacked there. Looking straight up above them I saw it – another small hole about three feet in diameter. I climbed up and shined my light inside.

This was going to be more difficult, and I prepared myself mentally for the next phase. I checked the twine, and there was still over a half-roll left, and I could see the trail I had left from it going back behind me to the last opening.

Then my flashlight went out.

I had experienced that degree of darkness a few times in my life. It was palpable and oppressing. The first feeling of fear hit me with such force that I could hardly think. I sat down on the floor of the cave and tried to gather my thoughts.

You've got batteries. You have another flashlight. Calm down.

I took several deep breaths and pulled my pack open. I felt for the extra flashlight and breathed a sigh of relief when it came on. I found the extra batteries and changed the ones in the first flashlight. Nothing. I changed the lamp and again had light. I stored the original batteries back into my pack. They were probably still good and would serve in a pinch. I placed the second light back into my pack and continued with the first one.

I climbed back up to the opening and wriggled inside. This time the passage was more difficult. Loose boulders had to be navigated around and over, and the general direction was upward at almost a forty-five degree angle. Rocks beneath my feet would slide and I would lose the few feet I had gained. I hoped that none of the ones that moved had blocked my return journey. It took nearly an hour to traverse the passage. When it opened up, I was looking at what first appeared to be empty space.

Then I realized that I was high up on a wall of another very large room, but it was below me. This one was huge, and I could hear water dripping. I shined the light down in front of me and could see that it was not a straight drop, but it would be a difficult climb down to the floor. Getting down was not my worry—getting back up was what nagged at the back of my mind.

I carefully turned around and started the downward climb. Rocks fell away frequently as I tried them for support. There was a large sturdy boulder protruding from the face so I took the time to fetch a rope from my pack and secured one end around it. Casting the rest down to the cave floor, I used it as support as I made my way down the rock face, feeling much more secure than I had without it.

According to my watch, two and one-half hours had elapsed since I had begun. Once I made it to the floor, I took a few minutes to rest and looked about the room. There was a large pool of water extending from the wall across from me, diminishing to a small stream that disappeared into the wall to my left. The floor was strewn with loose rock, some of them quite large. On the far wall to the right of the pool was a large expanse of flat, solid granite.

I moved closer.

There were symbols and drawings on it. Some hand outlines were there and what appeared to be drawings of animals, but they were faded with age. I recognized a deer, and what appeared to be a bear. There was a stick-man holding a spear, but I could make out little else.

I was not the first to see this place, and I knew that Keechie's brother and his father must have been here before me. But where could they have gone from here? Maybe Keechie's father had not gotten this far. I began studying the walls for additional openings.

Then I looked down at the floor. The sandy area near the edge of the pool caught my eye. I got down on my knees and looked more closely. There were small bare footprints leading right to the edge of the water. A second set of adult shoeprints was lying right alongside them.

Oh, no, I thought. *They went into the pool.*

Looking closer at the wall where the pool originated, I could see that it didn't come quite down to the water. There were several inches of clearance between the water surface and the wall opening. I pulled my pack off and lay it beside the pool, dreading what I was about to do.

I wrapped plastic around my flashlight and stepped cautiously into the pool, feeling cautiously for the bottom. It was only waist deep, but it was cold! I moved slowly toward the wall, crouching and ducking my head as I passed beneath the opening. Within several feet the ceiling opened up a bit and I could walk upright, but I was still waist deep in the icy water.

In less than twenty feet I came to another room. My first roll of twine was almost at the end of its length as I pulled myself up onto the bank of the pool. The extra twine was in my pack in the last room, but I wasn't going any further today. I just knew it. I had been very lucky so far and I didn't want to push it any further. If I had any more exploring to do, it was going to be right here in this room. There was always tomorrow.

I was shivering with cold as I surveyed my surroundings. It was almost as large as the last room, but the ceiling wasn't as high. The pool, now more like a wide stream, disappeared into the wall opposite me, but here there was no space between the surface of the water and the opening. I looked around the perimeter again.

There, just to the left of the passage I had just come through, was a depression in the rocks. I shined the light into it. There was sufficient room to crawl, so I went in a short way, and came to a dead end. I shined the light around and saw nothing, but just as I was about to turn and crawl back, something caught my eye.

It was just above my head and I moved closer. It was a shoe protruding from the wall! It was one of those work shoes like those my dad sold at the store. The local farmers called them "Brogans." I reached for it and it came off into my hand. A skeletal foot was exposed and I almost panicked, but rational thought took over. Right next to it was another shoe. I collected it too, seeing that it also had covered the bony remains of a foot.

I realized that I had just found George Washington, Keechie's missing father.

Chapter Six

George Washington Comes Home

As I made my way back through the tunnels, following the twine I had left, I tried to think of how I could break the news to Keechie. It may be a relief to know that he had not left them at all, but had died in a cave-in, still trying to find his son. When I finally arrived at the last tunnel, I could hear her calling.

"Is you alright, Brine? I hears you coming. Is dat you, Brine?"

I was almost at the opening and I answered, "Yep, it's me. I'm okay."

She was sitting at the edge of the pool when I emerged. She stood up and took my pack, then gave me a pat on the shoulder.

"I wuz so worried 'bout you, Brine. You sho gone a long time!"

"I was trying to be careful and taking my time, Keechie, and I found something..."

She heard the tone in my voice, and knew that it was not good.

"Didja find my brother, Brine?" she asked softly.

"No, not your brother, Keechie. But I found these." I pulled the brogans from my pack.

"Whut Pap's shoes doin' in dere?" she asked with a hint of panic in her voice.

"Are they your dad's for sure, Keechie?"

"Sho dey is. Onlest ones he ever had, fer as I knows."

"Then your father never left you, Keechie. I hate to tell you this, but he was killed in a rockslide up in the cave. He was probably still looking for your brother."

I then told her how I found the shoes, and that they were on the feet of a man—a skeleton actually, and that was all I could see due to the rockslide.

I caught Keechie as she crumpled toward the ground. She was sobbing.

"I done give 'im up fer det a long time ago. But all dis time I been a'hatin' 'im fer leavin' us. Now I knows he din' deserve no hate."

She paused for a long moment then said, "We gots t' get 'im outta dere, Brine. I gots t' give 'im a proper burral."

I knew there was no way I could talk her out of it, so I said, "I'll get him out, Keechie. I promise. But it will not be easy. Just moving any of those rocks may trigger another landslide."

"You ain't doin' it all by yoseff, Brine. I heps you. You needs t' rest now, but t'marra, we goes and gets 'im… please?"

I agreed, and then described to her the different passages we would have to go through —the climb down the rock wall, and the water pool with only inches for breathing.

"I kin make it, Brine. Iffen my li'l brother made it, I kin. Some thangs you juss gots t' do."

Keechie woke me early the next morning, and she was ready to go. We had a breakfast of grits and fried pork again which she prepared this time. She did it just as she had seen me do it, except for rinsing off the excess salt from the meat. It was way too salty for me, but she seemed to prefer it that way.

She had prepared herself a pack and had it slung over her shoulder in no time, rushing me toward the tunnel. We had brought candles to use at the cave-in site, to conserve the flashlight batteries.

The descent down the wall was easier this time since I had left the rope in place. When we arrived at the pool, Keechie showed the first sign of reluctance.

"May's well git a'goin'," she muttered. "Hit ain't gonna git no easier a'waitin'!"

I took of my shoes and placed them on the edge of the pool, and slipped into the cold water with Keechie right behind me.

"We ain' gotta put our heads unner the wada, do we Brine?" she asked nervously.

"Nevva did lak puttin' my head unner da wada."

"Nope, just lean your face up towards the ceiling. There's plenty of room there for breathing and it's not far. We'll be through in no time," I assured her, noticing how high the water came to her head, since she was so much shorter than I.

When we climbed out on the other side we lit several candles and extinguished the flashlight. I then pointed at the wall where her father lay buried beneath the rock. She went directly to it and lightly touched the bones of her father. Her lips moved, in a silent prayer, I supposed, so I left her alone until I heard her begin to move around.

"We've got to be very, very careful, Keechie. Moving any of these rocks could cause the rest to slide down on us. I think we should move the ones on top that may fall, and work our way down."

We rolled the ones we had moved out of the way and began working out way up into the collapsed tunnel. The bones had separated for the most part, and Keechie took them one by one as we reached them and placed them onto a blanket.

Fortunately for us, her father was lying at an angle of about forty-five degrees, so as we moved the rock we didn't have to go too far into the unstable tunnel, if it was a tunnel at all. It appeared that the wall itself had slid down, covering him. I hoped that he had been struck unconscious before he was buried. That was confirmed when we moved the last boulder from the skull—it was crushed at the crown.

He must have died instantly. We had found his left arm bones, but his right arm extended above his head, disappearing beneath the rocks. As I worked the last few larger ones from above us and passed them back to Keechie to roll out of our way, I felt the first movement begin.

"Back, Keechie, get back…. It's falling!" I shouted, but Keechie was already out of the way.

I slid and rolled away to the side just as a torrent of rocks slid into the opening we had just cleared.

"Whew, that was close!" I said as the dust slowly settled. "There could have been two more skeletons buried in here."

I looked at Keechie, whose eyes were as big as saucers.

We took a well-deserved break and ate the now soggy jerky I had brought. Keechie said that the water in the pool was safe to drink, but I drank from my canteen instead. I looked over at the wall where we had been working. There, right on top was the rest of her father's right arm.

Keechie went to gather it and suddenly cried, "Oh my Lawd, Brine. Look at DIS!"

I picked up a candle and went to her. She pointed at the skeletal hand, and then I looked closer.

Clasped within the skeletal fingers, were the bones of a small foot. George Washington had finally found his missing son.

That final rockslide had made our job much easier. The remains of Keechie's brother were mixed in among the top layer of stone. Everything that had fallen in on him had almost filled the space we had emptied. We removed the rubble and collected the bones. Keechie was careful to keep father and brother separated in her blanket, which now was quite bulky. She tied it up carefully for our return trip.

"He were jus' a couple o' y'ars younger'n me," she said as she tied the last cord around the bundle.

"Granny Boo say dat he were older'n his y'ars. Always trine t' be growed up, he wuz."

"What was his name, Keechie?"

"He never got his Injun man name, but Pap call him Little Gawg. 'Spose he were name afta Pap. His Injun name Mam give 'im were Stikini—hit mean 'L'il Screech Owl' in Injun."

Chapter Seven
The Burial

Gathering up our packs, we slid into the cold water and began our way back. When we got to the wall that we had to scale, I climbed up first. Keechie tied the packs to the rope and I hauled them up slowly. I then tossed the rope back down and told her to hang on while I helped pull her up. As I gathered the rope I re-coiled it, and we made our way back to her cave.

As we passed through one of the easier passages, I asked her, "How did you get your name, 'Keechie'?"

"Hee, hee, dat's what Pap call me. Mam give me da name 'Kachina', 'cause she say I looked lak one o' dem Kachina dolls de old 'uns brought hyer from out west. I'se so small she say I 'minded 'er o' dem. Pap juss shorten it t' Keechie"

That made sense to me. I had learned that the local Creek Indians had migrated into the area from the southwest, which agreed with what Keechie had told me. The Hopi and Navaho both had Kachina traditions in their religions. The word roughly translates into "Spirit

Being." The "Spirit Singers" of the tribe would contact the spirits, and the messages received from them were taught to the others by the use of the carved dolls, which represented the particular spirit contacted.

When we arrived back at the cave, Keechie let me stay at the hearth to change into dry clothes, while she changed in the storage room.

She had left a pot of water simmering on the hearth and she prepared us both a bowl of lemongrass and mint tea. It was good, but I made a mental note to add sugar to my list of things to bring her on my next trip.

She took the bones of her father and brother outside to dry, along with our wet clothes. She sat and watched as they lay in the sun, making sure no predators got at them, then cleaned them one at a time, murmuring prayers as she gently wiped each one.

She planned to bury them tomorrow, so I decided to stay with her one more night. I would have some explaining to do, but I had stayed away this long before. I knew that sooner or later I was going to have to tell my parents about Keechie, but first I had to convince Keechie that the times were different now. No one even had to know she was Indian, but with civil rights issues so prominent now, being black was more of a problem than being Indian. Times sure had changed since she was little!

Just before sunset, Keechie and I went to check on her rabbit traps. She made them by bending a sapling down, and attaching a noose to it. The bait was tied to the "trigger" stick and placed in the center of the noose, which held the sapling down. Any slight pull on the bait released the noose, hopefully capturing the rabbit in it.

We came back to the cave with two nice ones, each one large enough for two people to make a meal. I asked her if she would let me cook for us again. She smiled and agreed, but only if she cleaned them. She was worried that I would ruin the pelts!

I cut the dressed rabbit into frying sized pieces while the salt pork sizzled into enough grease to fry them in. I rolled the pieces in lightly salted and peppered cornmeal and started some beans boiling with a small piece of the pork.

I wasn't sure how the cornmeal would do without an egg, but I had no choice. Keechie took the remaining rabbit and cut the flesh into thin strips, and hung them above the fire on long green twigs to smoke. I had never tried rabbit jerky.

The rabbit was done long before the beans, but it was delicious! Keechie loved it.

"Ain't never had no rabbit fried in poke grease befo'. Makes it taste lak boff! Hee, hee."

I showed her how my mom saved the grease so it could be used again.

"My Mam say dey usta do dat wit bear grease, but I ain't nevva seed no bear 'roun' hyer. Granny Boo say dat da men usta go up nawth to get bear. I'se got some bear robes in da otha room. One a' dem wuz my Grampa's."

It was getting dark in the cave, so I lit one of the lamps. Keechie was sewing the bones of her father and brother into rawhide bundles, and I was watching silently, giving her time to grieve. The fire felt good and I soon dozed off sitting front of the hearth.

While I was napping, Keechie had spread out the sleeping blankets.

"We's best get us some sleep, Brine, 'cause I wants to be at the burral ground at sunrise."

She added green hickory wood to the coals to smoke the rabbit strips while we slept.

She was already dressed when I awoke. She was in full Indian dress – wearing a soft, almost white shirt and dress, both decorated with beads and quills. Her braided hair was in one long ponytail, held by a silver and turquoise clasp. She was wearing a beautiful matching necklace and she caught me staring at it.

"Hit were Granny Boo's," she said. "Hit's been in da fambly fer years. Come from out west, she say."

I had seen others like it called "Squash blossom" that were made by the Navajo silversmiths of the midwest.

I dressed quickly and we were at the rock before sunup. Keechie insisted on carrying the burial bundles herself, so I carried her small drum and gourd rattles she had brought with her.

"Dey's fer waking the Spirits," she told me. "Gots t' get dey attention sometimes, spechully when you burrin' da dead. We usta keep a fire burnin' an' stay at dey grave fer fo days. But wid us hidin' out an' all, we hat t' change dat custom. Cain't have no far fer dat long less'n hit get seed "

We cleared out a space between two large boulders on the face of the mountain. Just as the sun was rising she began striking the drum slowly and softly, chanting as I had heard her when we visited here before. She had me to sit and shake the gourd rattles in time with her drumming.

I found myself entranced by the ancient ceremony as she shuffle-stepped in front of the boulders, beating the drum louder and louder and increasing the tempo as she did. With a staccato flourish, she threw back her head and gave a shrill, ululating cry to the sky.

She then placed the drum beside me on the ground and gathered the bundles of her dad and brother. She placed them deeply into the space between the boulders, and I helped place stones in front of them. We finished by placing a large boulder over the space, moving it about until it looked natural. The burial was complete.

Chapter Eight
Keechie's 50th Year Anniversary Outing

As we made our way slowly back to the cave, I asked Keechie how she felt about going for a ride in my car, and maybe even going for a trip into town.

"There's nothing to fear, Keechie. You won't even be noticed these days. Times have changed."

"I be a'skeered, Brine, but I sho wants to. I wants to see people up close. I wants to look at the stuff in da sto's, an' ride inna car, an'…"

She paused abruptly and grinned from ear to ear.

"Guess I got carr'd 'way thar fer a minnit. I been thankin' 'bout dat fer nigh on fifty yars!"

I was thrilled. She wanted to go! This would make it easier for me to tell my parents about her, and I was needing to tell them something other than, "I'm going camping" since these trips to Keechie's cave were getting rather frequent. My friends were even getting suspicious, since I had just gotten a car and was hardly using it.

"I'll go home today and get my car. I'll meet you at the top of the rock. You can wear what you're wearing now if you want to!"

I gathered up my stuff back at the cave and left immediately. This was going to be an adventure for the both of us!

"If something happens and I don't come back today, it'll be because my mom is mad at me for staying so long, but I think it'll be okay. If I don't come today, then it'll be tomorrow. Do you understand, Keechie? I'll be back today if everything is okay at home, I promise."

Mom was upset with me, but was so glad I was okay that she didn't ground me. I took a shower, changed clothes and told her I was going to Chipley just to ride around.

Around two in the afternoon, I was back at the Rock, and Keechie was waiting. She was still dressed in her Indian clothing, looking very elegant. I got out and opened the passenger door for her and she slowly got in, but she was obviously nervous as she slid into the seat. I closed the door and went around and got into the driver's seat. Before I started the engine, I turned on the radio.

She jumped as the music blared out, but laughed when she realized what it was.

"I heerd dat befo', when I went down t' da houses, and when Pap took me t' town," she said through her laughter.

"I'm going to start the engine now, Keechie. It's what makes the car go."

I cranked the motor and put it in gear. She gripped the dashboard as I pulled out onto the road. I drove slowly and began making comments about the scenery, trying to get her to relax a bit. It worked. There were several places cleared along the roadside that offered good scenic views of the valley below, and I pulled into each one briefly so she could take in the view.

As we neared the turn down the mountain towards Chipley, I told her that this was the site of an old stagecoach stop called "King's Crossing."

"He was an old Indian named King, and he ran the place. Even the intersection here is named 'King's Gap' for him."

"I heerd my Granny Boo say dat name befo'. I thank he wuz a brother er cousin to Bull Killer's father. He wuz one a' da ones who leff when da sojers come."

I made the turn and we began down the opposite side of the mountain from Keechie's cave. The land leveled out and cleared fields came into view, but it was the many fences that got her attention.

"My Pap say dat de white man build fences 'roun' evathang, 'vidin' up de lan' so's no one else kin cross it."

"They are mostly to keep the livestock in, Keechie, but the results are the same."

Chipley was almost deserted when we got there.

Good thing, I thought. *Better to not confront her with a crowd on her first trip.*

I drove around the main part of town and told her what the different buildings were. None of the buildings in this sleepy little country town was over two stories, but it was a new world to her. Even the power lines and streetlights were things of wonder.

I pulled into a parking space outside the Thrift Store.

"Let's go in here and look around, Keechie. They got a little bit of everything in here, clothes, shoes, cooking stuff... everything!"

I went around the car and opened the door for her. She appeared to be getting nervous again, but I grabbed her arm and gave her a smile.

"It's okay, Keechie. You'll like it!"

There were only two or three customers inside, and about the same number of staff members. No one even looked our way, but Keechie hung back, her eyes darting all over the store. I grabbed a shopping cart and directed her back to the appliance section.

I picked up a twelve-inch iron skillet, complete with lid, and checked the price—seventy-five cents. I placed it in the cart.

Keechie was getting into this now. She was staring at the utensils heaped into a tray. Knives, forks and spoons of various types and designs overflowed in a jumble.

She picked up one of the table knives, felt the edge and said, "Dese ain't even sharp, but they sho is purdy!"

"Those are butter knives, Keechie. They're not used for cutting that much. People use them for spreading stuff on bread."

"Hmph, don't need no spechul knife fer dat. But dese…" she said as she picked up a fork, "Pap usta have one o' dese. Say dat de only thang he missed when he wuz a'eatin' Mam's cookin'."

"Pick out some you like, Keechie," I told her. They were only a nickel each. She rummaged through the pile and found three that matched.

I found three tablespoons that were the same pattern and placed them in the cart.

"Got to have enough for company," I joked.

We made our way through the store. She was more intent on just looking at everything. She had no need for accessories, since she had survived this long without them. In fact, she seemed to find it amusing that people thought they needed these things!

I led her back to the clothing section for girls. I figured she was about the same size as a twelve or thirteen year-old and showed her the blouses and dresses that I thought would fit her.

Now she took on more interest. She felt of everything. She looked inside at the seams, apparently judging the construction method. She was especially attracted to the floral patterned dresses, so I held one of them up to her and asked if she would like to try it on.

"Right hyer?" she asked with alarm.

"No, they've got a special room for that, right over there," I told her and pointed.

"Pick out three or four you like and take them in there with you and try them on."

Just then one of the other customers, a white lady, passed by us and said, "That's a simply LOVELY dress, dear," pointing at Keechie's rawhide dress. "Where EVER did you find it?"

Keechie was stunned, but stammered, "I foun' it on da deer, but I made it myseff!"

I believe the woman thought Keechie was joking with her, but said, "Well, it's just lovely, dear. I just LOVE Indian costume," and moved along.

Keechie and I looked at each other for a moment and suddenly we both burst out in laughter. All the apprehension and tension we had built up poured out in peals of sidesplitting laughter.

She finally recovered enough to say, "I go tries dese on now," as she wiped her eyes.

I waited outside the door to the changing room as she tried on the dresses. Several minutes passed and I was about to call to her, but from inside came an annoyed voice.

"How dey 'speck you ta work dis thang in da back?"

I realized that she was having trouble with the zipper, then remembered that she didn't have anything that used them, then wondered if she had ever even SEEN one.

"Just come to the door and I'll zip you," I said.

She backed up to the door and I reached in and zipped the back of the dress.

"You'll get used to it, my friend. Everyone has the same problem."

"Dey all fits, I reckon, but dat zippa thang ain't sompin' I wants to have t' larn."

She looked like a little girl for sure now. The floral-printed dress was just right for her and I said so.

"Hee, hee. I feels lak a little gurl, too. 'Bout the same size, anyways. M' ol' bones tell a differnt story…"

I helped her pick out some plain, slip-on shoes and we went to the checkout counter. The total was only seven dollars and change. Keechie watched with interest as I handed the clerk the money.

"Pap leff a lot o' dat when he… went missin'. I gots it inna jar in da sto' room. Ain't nevva hat no use fer it."

We were walking out the door as I asked, "You've had money all these years and didn't spend it, Keechie?"

"Warn't goin' t' town by myseff, and I juss din' need nothin'."

As we drove back to the rock, I mentally calculated Keechie's age, and the approximate year of her birth. If she was fifty when Granny Boo had died, and that was ten years ago, and the year was now 1958… she must have been born just before the turn of the century—around 1898 or so. The money her father had left her must be from before 1898 until about 1908, if she had been around ten when he "left." The coins, and bills if there were any, would probably have some collector value in additional to their face value.

"Why did your father save the money, Keechie, instead of spending it?"

"He say he din' need no more'n 'e had, an' 'e wanted t' send me an' my brother off t' school. We din' wanna leave, an' 'sides, dey wern't no schools 'roun' hyer fer Injuns. Den 'e were gone, so's dat wuz dat."

"He sounds like a good father, Keechie. Where was he from?"

"He say 'is fokes wuz slaves down in Lu-Zanna. Dey got freed, but dere warn't no work fer 'em, 'ceptin' what dey wuz already doin' – workin' in da cane fields. Dat's whut 'e leff behin'," she said as she looked out the window, watching the landscape go by.

"He were borned free, but dey wuz treated turrble. May's well still be slaves, 'e say."

"Will you show me what he left, Keechie"?

"Sho, I shows ya. You can have it, all I keer. Ain't doin' me no good. Don' need it no more'n 'e did. Pays ya back fer da stuff ya done brung me."

I walked back with her down the mountainside to her cave. It was late afternoon and I had to leave soon. I was still not in my mom's best graces, and dad would have something to say too. I just felt it.

"Can I tell my folks about you, Keechie? They want to know what I've been up to, and I think they will like you anyway. Besides, we don't have to tell them where you live if you don't want to."

"Sho, you kin tells 'em. Dey must be nice fokes t' raise a boy lak you," she said with a hint of a smile.

There was concern written there too, but I figured that was from the years of secrecy she had lived through. I was trying to lead her into the modern world as gently and slowly as I could. I had read articles in *National Geographic* that talked about newly discovered tribes in South America experiencing "Culture Shock" when first introduced to modern society. I wanted only the best for Keechie, and I was afraid for her.

As soon as we reached the cave we went inside. She pulled a few strips of the rabbit jerky from the hearth and passed some to me. She went into the other room and came back with a gourd of water and a large, heavy pottery jar. She set the jar down and handed me the gourd.

"Wish I hat 'membered to salt it," she said as she chewed the jerky.

"Hit sho need salt!"

"It's good to me just like it is, but it could use some spice," I replied, drinking deeply from the gourd.

She put away her new clothes and picked up the jar of her dad's money.

"Dis whut he leff," she said as she handed it to me.

"I walks wit' ya t' da rock. Yo Mam prolly be worrin' 'bout you."

We said our goodbyes at the base of the rock and she thanked me for the day and the clothes. She held her arms out to me as if about to give me a hug, but once again took my shoulders in her hands and gave them a squeeze. She was still watching me as I reached the top and turned to wave to her.

This woman had become a very important part of my life.

Chapter Nine
George Washington's Treasure

The pottery jar that she had given me containing her Dad's money was very heavy. I guessed that it contained mostly coins, and I had an idea that there may be more value to them as collector pieces. I couldn't wait to get to my room and check out the contents, but first I had to face my parents. I wanted a few more days with Keechie before school started.

In addition, bow season was going to open on my last weekend. I didn't want to be grounded and miss that! I had been bow hunting for deer for the past two years and had gotten pretty good at it.

Deer had become scarce around here since farming had caused most of them to leave. Plans were to "plant" deer back into the county but the larger farmers had objected. Fences didn't stop deer as well as they did cattle, and deer loved young tender shoots of almost anything that was planted.

Entering our house through the back door, so I could quickly stash the jar in my closet, I almost ran into my mom. I had frightened her, but luckily that caused her to miss what I was carrying.

"Gotta put my stuff away, Mom. What's for supper?"

"Your dad's bringing chicken home from the store. He wants you to start the grill so it'll be ready when he gets here. You nearly scared the life outta me. Why didn't you come in the front door?"

Before I could think of an answer, she said, "Oh, and get the grill started, he'll be home in about thirty minutes."

"Okay, Mom, I'll start it now."

I hid the jar in my closet, and went out and grabbed the charcoal and lighter fluid. I placed the charcoal into a pyramid like he taught me, doused it with the fluid and soon had a towering flame going.

Dad loved to barbecue chicken, and he developed his own method and his own secret sauce. He had a reputation as the best chicken barbequer around. The coals had to be just right before he would even put the chicken halves on.

I went back into the kitchen where Mom was getting everything else ready, and sat down at the table, trying to figure out how to bring up the subject of Keechie. I decided on the direct route.

"Mom, I met an old Indian woman. She lives all alone up near the mountain. Did you ever know of any Indians around here?"

"Well, no, come to think of it. I don't think I've ever even SEEN an Indian except those up in North Georgia where we went on vacation last year."

We had gone up to the Blue Ridge Mountains and stopped at a Cherokee festival that was part of the Georgia State Mountain Fair. There were some real Indians there, but they were so theatrical, dressed up in full war paint and long, very fake headdresses, it was hard to think of them as real Indians. They were selling fake tomahawks, fake jewelry and fake Indian blankets (Made in Taiwan). They were not very convincing as far as I was concerned.

"Well, this woman is more than half Indian. Her daddy was a black man. Her mother and grandmother were full-blooded Creek Indians from around here, but that was before the soldiers made them leave. Her family stayed though, and she has been hiding up on the mountain for all these years. Her family is all gone, and she's been there all alone for years."

That should be enough information for now, I thought. Just one more question remained...

"Wanna meet her?"

"Is she here?" Mom asked, looking past me towards the back door.

"No, she's not here now. She's afraid to leave her place, since she isn't used to people much. She sure knows how to survive on her own though."

"She sounds very interesting, Brian. I think I would like to meet her."

What do you think Dad would say?"

I was afraid of the answer, because I knew the "black father" part would be his problem with allowing her in his home as a guest. He would be civil, and if she were a customer in his store, he would treat her as cordially as he would anyone else—but to have a black guest in our home was usually out of the question. To my father's generation, any black blood at all in your heritage made you black. Lightness of skin or percentage of mixture did not matter at that point.

"You know how he is, Brian. As long as he doesn't have to eat with her... you know."

It was true. Frequently we would have a maid to come in to help with the housework. It was okay for her to prepare our meals, but it was NOT acceptable to eat at the same table at the same time. It just wasn't done.

I never felt right with the racial prejudices I grew up around. It just seemed so... wrong, somehow; but this was his house, and we followed his rules.

"Maybe I'll bring her over when Dad's at work, and let her meet you first. She's really a neat lady. She knows a lot about wild herbs and natural remedies and stuff like that. Kinda like the things Granny Barnes knows, except a lot more."

"She's never even been in a real house before," I slipped.

Oops, that was a mistake, I thought, and Mom caught it.

"What do you mean… a REAL house, Brian?"

"Well, you know, one with electricity, and lights, and television—stuff like that," I quickly ad-libbed.

Dang, that was close.

I wasn't ready to tell her that she lived in a cave. She wouldn't understand how well Keechie got by NOT having all those things… but living in a cave? That would be asking too much for her to accept all at once

"Ohhh, no electricity? How does she keep her food cold? How does she keep up with what's going on in the world, with no radio or television?"

"Well, she smokes and dries her meat, and eats fresh vegetables, and she dries her beans and corn, and that kind of stuff… you know—like they did in the pioneer days."

"Oh, okay. Poor soul. It must be hard, not having a refrigerator…"

"She does pretty well from what I've seen, Mom. Can I bring her for a visit?

"Sure, okay, bring her by this weekend—on Saturday. I'll fix us a good dinner and we can talk. I really would like to meet her."

Dad drove up just as we finished talking. I went out to check on the coals in the grill. In a few minutes, he came out the back door with the chicken halves on a tray in one hand and a beer in the other.

"Hi, son. Fire ready? Throw these on while I go start the sauce."

He always made the sauce himself. We all knew the "secret" recipe, but he always wanted to do it personally. In several more minutes he came back out to check on the fire.

"Looks good, boy. You're learning!"

The coals were almost burned up, with white ashes covering the top, just when the heat is at its peak. The chicken was always started cut side up, to get the grill marks on them. Then they were turned over for the remainder of the cooking.

He pulled up his favorite lawn chair next to the grill and sat down. He had his spray bottle of water that he used to extinguish the flare-ups from the dripping fat.

Dad worked six days a week at the store, usually ten to twelve hours a day, and, having worked there myself, I knew how tired your feet and legs could get. He had done it for all my sixteen years of life, and had done it a few years before that.

We chit-chatted about little things while the chicken was cooking—school starting next week, bow season… stuff like that.

"Going hunting next weekend, son? Mr. Hancock said he's seen several deer over at his place this year. Said we could hunt his land if we want to."

Mr. Hancock lived fairly close to the mountain, maybe two miles north of where Keechie's cave was.

"Sure would like to get me another big buck this year, Dad. Can you come with me?"

He was an excellent marksman with a rifle, but had never hunted with a bow. He hardly ever got a chance to go anyway, but the few times he had gone during gun season, he had killed a deer.

My folks didn't like venison as much as I did, so he always gave it away. But he knew how to dress a deer. Being a butcher, he would cut it up expertly before offering it to his friends.

"Can't go this year, but maybe Mr. Hancock or his boys will go with you. He says the deer have been in his cornfield all summer. He wants them gone anyway."

I preferred going bowhunting alone, and if I got one, I was going to give it to Keechie to help her through the winter. She would be impressed if I killed her a deer with the same type of weapon that had originated with her people.

Mom came to the door and announced that everything else was ready.

"How's the chicken coming along?" she asked.

"Just putting the sauce on, honey. Five minutes and one more beer, please," dad answered.

Chicken usually takes an hour and a half to barbecue properly, so we must have been talking that long. I really loved to have these talks with him. Kinda man-to-man talk. I admired him for his dedication to his job, but regretted not having him go hunting and fishing with me. I knew he would have loved to do those things, but he never seemed to have the time. The store and providing for his family had always come first.

We had a wonderful meal – barbecued chicken, baked potatoes, cole slaw and baked beans. Afterwards, Dad moved into the living room to watch Walter Cronkite, his favorite news commentator.

Mom began cleaning up the supper dishes, and I went to my room to check out the contents of George Washington's pottery jar of money, which was now mine,

I emptied the jar onto my bed where I could quickly cover it with a blanket, and stashed the large vessel back into my closet. There were a LOT of coins there, and many bills—more than I had imagined.

I began by sorting the coins out by denomination, but noticed at once that they were very old, just as I had guessed. The nickels varied from the "Buffalo" ones to the older "V" nickels. Now I was getting excited. I had begun collecting coins early in life and had a book on coin collecting, and these were promising to be more collectible than I had ever guessed.

Then I came to the pennies. There were many of the old "Large Cent" pieces, and even more of the "Indian Head" ones. Some particular dates, I knew, were very rare. I raked my hand across the unsorted pile and there, gleaming with that radiance that only gold can give, were several large gold coins—"Twenty Dollar" gems of highly desirable, very collectible and very valuable gold pieces.

I was stunned. My heart was racing and my mouth became dry as I separated them out of the pile. Then I noticed that many of the smaller sized coins were also gold. I began sorting all the coins according to their denomination.

All the paper money was folded tightly. As I separated the folds, I saw that they were apparently from different "pay periods", since the folded bundles contained twenties, tens and singles – usually totaling sixty to eighty dollars each, and there were many bundles of the bills.

I had a friend in LaGrange whose father owned a small

"Collectibles" shop, but specialized in coins—numismatics, he called it. I decided to take one coin and one bill of each different date and denomination to him for appraisal. That way, I could get an idea of the value of George Washington's "treasure" without disclosing the entire collection. I then added up the face value of the pile on my bed.

It was just over twenty-five thousand dollars!

Chapter Ten
Deer Hunter

There was a mist hanging above the spring when I arrived at dawn, and I almost expected to see Keechie there again, like the first day I met her. She had shown me deer sign at one of her corn patches nearby. There were trees on the perimeter of her field that showed signs of where the bucks had rubbed their antlers, and I was heading there. I had already picked out a tree to climb and wait.

If I hadn't known the area so well I could have never made it in the dim pre-dawn light. I checked the light breeze and approached the open area from downwind, in case there were deer already there that could pick up my scent. I quickly scaled the tree up to a large limb that made a convenient resting place. I strung my bow, selected an arrow, and began the wait.

Just at sunup, I saw the first doe on the far side of the open area in front of me. She was staying in the shadows, and sniffing the morning air. Then another, then a third doe appeared. They moved onto the edge of the clearing and began alternating between grazing and lifting their heads to sniff the air.

During bow season you could take either buck or doe, but I wanted a buck to give Keechie. Besides, the deer population was too low, and leaving the does made more sense.

As the morning progressed, the breeze shifted and I was concerned that it would carry my scent directly to them. A slight noise from my left caused me to freeze.

I caught a small movement in my peripheral vision, and then watched as the huge buck made his way cautiously into the field. He had apparently circled the clearing, and was now approaching his harem. When he was about twenty yards in front of me, he paused and turned, raising his nose to the wind.

A gunshot rang out in the distance, echoing through the valley. The buck went into full alert as I nocked the arrow, drew it fully, took a deep breath and let it fly.

The arrow struck him just behind his right shoulder. It looked like a perfect shot! He stumbled once then went down. I nocked another arrow just in case, but I knew that he was mortally wounded, if not already dead.

The doe were gone into the cover of the woods in two bounds.

As I made my way down the tree, I froze again. Crashing through the underbrush, in the same path the buck had taken, came a screeching apparition that looked vaguely like…

Keechie! She had her knife in her hand, laughing and hollering as she approached the downed buck.

"Hee, hee, heeeeeee, Brine! Come on down hyer. We got's t' get 'im blooded. That wuz a fine shot! Yo be an Injun fer sho!"

She grabbed the buck by the antlers, pulling his head back, and drove her knife down into the "Vee" of his neck, severing the jugular veins, allowing the blood to run out freely.

It was the same method I used, and I said so.

"But Where did you come from, Keechie? I thought I was all alone out here!"

"Hee, hee, I'se been follerin' you since you leff de sprang. When

I seed dat bow, I kinda figgered whut you wuz up to. De wind 'most gave you 'way dere. Course you uz up in dat tree, so's you might a been okay."

We dragged the deer to a tree, and hoisted him up by his back legs in order to field dress him. Keechie asked if I knew about the scent glands. I called them the musk glands, but I told her I knew about them. Not removing them or not doing it properly would spoil the meat.

She deftly took care of them, but instead of throwing them away, she set them aside for some reason. She helped with the field dressing and the removing of the internal organs, chanting and thanking the deer's spirit for his offering of meat as she worked. I joined her with my own offering of appreciation.

She took the liver and cut a small piece, which she cut in two halves. Looking me dead in the eyes, she solemnly offered one of the halves to me. I had never eaten raw liver before, or any other part of a deer for that matter, but I realized that she was doing a ceremonial thing.

I took it into my mouth, tasted briefly and swallowed. She took the other half and chewed slowly, apparently savoring the taste.

"First meat go t' da hunter. He make de kill. He get first taste," she said solemnly. "Whatcha gone do wit da meat, Brine? Yo fokes lak deer meat?"

"I wanted you to have it, Keechie, to help you get through the winter. I was going to surprise you."

"Well, you sho already done dat, killing dis fine buck wit' a bow n' arrow! I figgered you use a gun, lak Pap did. Granny Boo say she could tell da differnce 'tween a bow kill n' a gun kill. I thank she right. Don' know why."

We went ahead and dressed the deer fully since Keechie wanted the hide. Keechie cut my arrow out and handed it to me.

"Right through da heart, Brine. Perfek shot!" she informed me. We quartered the carcass to make transporting it easier. I figured it dressed out about a hundred pounds and would take two trips to get the meat back to the cave.

We buried the offal but left some organs for scavengers. I hoisted the two remaining quarters up into the tree for safekeeping, and we headed back to the cave.

As soon as we arrived, Keechie began cutting the meat up, apparently to make jerky, so I went back for the remaining meat. As I walked, I thought about the way she had found me. It seemed that nothing moved in these woods without her knowing it.

Nearing the clearing, I heard voices. I immediately went down to my knees, and listened.

"I swear I heard talking over here," I heard one of them say. I recognized the voice. It was Mr. Hancock's son, Billy Joe. I stood back up and approached them.

"Hi, guys, I said as I approached them. It was the two brothers, Billy Joe and Tim Junior.

They both jumped and Billy Joe asked, "What you doing out here, Brian?"

I already got one, Billy Joe. Y'all have any luck?"

"Well, I shot me a doe this morning, but she ran. We tracked her near here, but then lost the trail. What did you get?"

"A big buck. Got the rest of him up in that tree. I already took the rest back."

"Bet you done got my deer, Brian," he said. I couldn't tell if he was serious or not, but luckily I had left the head with the antlers here to bring back later.

"You say you shot a doe, right?" I asked as I went to the tree where I had left the two quarters.

"Yep. Big ol' doe, too. She probably dead by now, somewhere 'roun' here. If it ain't the one you got..." he said.

"Not unless the does are growing these now," I told him as I lifted the head with the full set of antlers up from beneath the tree.

"I'll help you find yours, though. It would be a shame to let one get away that's wounded. How come you didn't use a bow? It's not gun season yet."

"Law says we can shoot 'em on our own property if they're

causing a problem… and they's a problem. I ain't hunting her any more either. Let the buzzards have 'er, all I care. We don't even like venison. I just like shooting them."

I couldn't believe what I was hearing, but then again, coming from him, I believed it. His dad was different, and would never let an animal suffer, but his boys were a different story.

After they left I made a circle around the clearing. On the northern edge towards their farm, I found a patch of blood. I saw the tracks leading towards the mountain and followed them. About ten yards further there was more blood, and the tracks now became obvious. It was dragging at least one leg, which made the trail easier to follow.

I found her in a tangle of honeysuckle. She was almost dead, but still trying to get up. I nocked another arrow and shot her straight from the front just at the collarbone. Her eyes glazed over as she died instantly. I cut her jugular and dragged her back to the clearing about a hundred yards away as the crow flies.

The bullet wound was apparent. She had been gut-shot and would have suffered several hours before she died. She was probably one of the same herd that I had seen this morning, but she was young, probably no more than two years.

I lowered the meat I had stashed earlier and hoisted her up with the same rope. I did a quick field dressing and left her there while I went back for Keechie. At least the meat would not be wasted.

She was just about finished with the first half when I got there. Most of the meat was in thin strips for jerking, but there were several large cuts that she would use for roasts and steaks.

I told her about the Hancock boys and the doe they had wounded, and I had finished off.

"Woowie, now we gots mo meat than we need. I heerd dat gunshot. Reckon I kin get away wit' an outside far to smoke 'em on, Brine? Don' wanna 'track no 'tention, iffen I don' haff to."

"I think a fire would be alright, Keechie. They don't live that close, and they aren't very observant; and besides, they're lazy!" I quipped.

We went back to the clearing and finished dressing the doe. She was small enough that we were able to carry all the meat back in one trip, along with the rack from my buck, but Keechie was determined to bring both hides back to the cave to tan. I made the additional trip for her.

Then I helped her cut up the remainder of the two kills and soon had the majority of the jerky strips smoking over two fires. The sun would do the rest after an initial smoking. This time we used salt and some other herbs to flavor the meat.

I carried the two hindquarters from the doe home with me that afternoon and Mom helped me prepare them for slow cooking on the grill we used for smoking. We removed all the fat from the meat and inserted pork tallow deep into the roasts. It would be difficult to tell the difference between venison and a pork roast when prepared this way.

"Your dad will be proud of you, Brian. You got a deer with your bow!"

I didn't tell her that I had actually killed two deer today, even though one had been an act of mercy, so I just left the comment unanswered.

"I gave the rest of the meat away, mom… to Keechie. She likes venison."

Chapter Eleven
Keechie and Mom

The next day was Saturday, and I wanted to get an early start. Keechie and I had planned the day for her visit with my mom, and I was excited and just a little bit nervous about it. I awoke early but Mom was already busy straightening up the house for the visit, although I had kept reminding her that Keechie had nothing to compare it with.

"She's never even been in a house with electricity, Mom. Where she lives would be considered a cave compared to here anyway," I said with a smile at my private, yet truthful joke.

Keechie met me at the top of the rock, dressed in one of the new dresses I had bought her. She looked wonderful, but she was even more nervous than my mom.

"I ain't never been a'vistin' befo', Brine. What iffen she don' lak me? What us gonna talk 'bout, anyhow? I cain't even talk right, you know, lak a lady talk to another lady. We don' have nuthin' da same as…"

"Keechie!" I interrupted. "She knows about you. She was interested in how you live, how you have survived all these years without a refrigerator. She wants to meet you. You will like her, and she will like you. Don't worry so much, okay? Tell her about your family, your Granny Boo, and how she taught you about the herbs. Mom likes to learn about herbs. Remember, her mother, my Granny Barnes, was pretty good with them too!"

I drove slowly down the mountain, giving her time to adjust to the idea of meeting a white woman who lived in a house with a refrigerator, not to mention a television and a telephone.

Mom was waiting on the porch when we pulled into the driveway. She met us halfway to the house with a warm welcome.

"Hi, Miss Keechie. Brian has told me an awful lot about you, but he didn't tell me how pretty you were," and took her hand in hers.

The tension seemed to ease between them. Mom had done exactly the right thing at exactly the right moment.

"Brine din' tell me whut t' calls you, Missus…" Keechie said, looking at me with accusation.

"Call me Ginnie, Keechie. It's short for Virginia, just like Keechie is short for Kachina. Brian told me about your name," Mom replied with just the right answer. I was so proud of her.

Just as we entered the house, the telephone rang. Keechie jumped and looked around wildly. Mom just laughed and picked up the receiver. She spoke a few words and hung up.

"Just your grandma, Brian. She'll call back later."

My grandmother was about the same age as Keechie and lived a few miles away in the same community.

"Where she at, Brine?" Keechie asked, looking about the room.

I explained to her as well as I could about telephones—wires that you could talk over for great distances, but I saw that she had already placed them in the category of magic, so I let the subject drop. I would try to explain in detail later. She still had television to see for the first time, after all.

Mom invited her into the kitchen, where most of our family discussions took place—sitting at the table with tea or coffee.

Keechie walked slowly around the room, taking in all the appliances and utensils.

Mom put on a pot of tea to boil and lit the gas eye on the stove. It had one of the newer pilot lights that ignited automatically by just turning on the gas. Keechie was amazed, but remained silent. She gave me a look that said, "Tell me later."

"Show me dat... frigerater, Brine. Dat box what keep food cole."

"Right here, Keechie," I said as I opened the door. "Feel the cold?"

She placed her head inside, and as her eyes scanned the contents, said, "Hit be lak winner in dere! Lectricty do dat too?"

"Yep. It's all done with electricity, Keechie, and when it goes out, we don't have any way to keep the food. Your way is best when that happens!"

Mom had her sit at the table as she prepared the tea. We usually drank iced, sweet tea, but mom always liked to have hot tea for guests. We had an herb garden with several varieties of mint, and she loved to experiment with them.

Keechie smelled the aroma and recognized it at once. "I gots somma dat mint myseff," she said with glee.

"Hit's one a' my favrites."

She and mom immediately began talking about the different mints, then the different herbs they both grew and/or knew about. Keechie forgot all about her reservations about meeting another woman. She was now in her element.

Mom told her that her mother would also be interested in her knowledge of herbal medicines, since that was where she learned what little she knew about them.

"The two of you would hit it off immediately, Keechie. She knows more about their medicinal uses. I mostly just cook with them."

Mom learned of their culinary value since we had access to store-bought medicines, but Grandma Barnes used them for medicinal purposes in times when there was nothing else available. She even referred to them as "Injun Medicine."

The afternoon went by all too quickly. Mom was really enjoying Keechie's company, and Keechie was opening up as I had never seen her do before. They both seemed to share the mutual pleasure of another woman's company, but for Keechie, it was fulfilling something that she had missed for most of her life. The differences in ages, races, cultures and lifestyles fell away as the two women found common ground in which to interact.

I felt very proud of them both, so I just remained silent for the most part, and enjoyed their spirited conversation.

Mom prepared a light lunch for us of ham and tomato sandwiches, which Keechie found delicious, never having had sliced bread or mayonnaise. The iced tea came out, but Keechie was more fascinated by the ice cubes than she was by the sweetened tea.

When it was time for us to leave and get Keechie back to her cave, Mom invited her to come back.

"Anytime, Keechie. You will always be welcome here, and I want you to meet Brian's dad. I'm sure he will want to meet you too!"

She followed us out to the driveway and took Keechie's hands in hers.

"Please come back to see us, Keechie. I really enjoyed the day with you."

I gave Mom a hug and whispered to her, "Thanks, Mom, for making Keechie feel welcome."

On the way back up the mountain I pointed out the telephone and power lines that carried the voices and electricity to the houses, and tried to explain to her how it worked.

"It's not magic, Keechie, it's just technology."

"Hit's magic to me, Brine, Pyo magic!" she said with a happy, contented smile. She had enjoyed the day, and I hoped that there would be many more like it.

Chapter Twelve
Keechie and Puma Man

Entering her cave after her day with Brian and his mom, Keechie felt torn between conflicting emotions. She was still elated over the visit. Brian's mom had made her feel completely at home in the strange environment, and they had shared what only women can share, and that was mostly on an emotional level that no words can explain. They also shared common interests in herbs used in cooking and for medicine.

Sho would lak to meet Brine's Granny. Iffen she wants to know 'bout medison, we has a lot to talk 'bout.

But what occupied most of her emotional state was that she realized just how much she had missed people. She spent so much time alone and become so attuned to her way of life, that she had forgotten what interacting with others felt like.

She took a chance with Brian, but her spirit guide told her to speak to him that day at the spring. Maybe this was what the Puma Man intended—to lead her into connecting with society again.

She lit one of the lamps that Brian had brought her and carried it into the storage room where she stood, gazing at her family's possessions. The memories washed over her as she lightly touched each article.

When she touched Granny Boo's Power Bundle, the jolt was instantaneous; but it was clear in its intention. She took it down from the wall, placed it around her neck, and returned to her sleeping furs in front of the hearth.

She sat and stared at the embers in the fireplace, letting the feelings wash over her. Keechie was accustomed to the ways of the spirit world, and was familiar with it. She was Shaman.

Few spiritwalkers had ever held the position without having a tribe to acknowledge it. This fact alone had allowed her to surpass most, if not all of her predecessors, but she had no way of knowing or comparing that.

Granny Boo was there, smiling lovingly and pointing at her head.
"look inside, little Keechie girl. Let the spirits guide you like I taught you. Your Mam did not have the Gift, but you do. Look to the Puma man. He will show you..."

At once, the vision changed and Keechie went deeper into trance. Puma was there, with his cat eyes looking deeply into her soul. She had seen him many times in her life, and had never been afraid. He spread his arms wide, then turned, offering his huge back for her to mount.

Keechie was at once astride, and almost simultaneously, they were flying high above her cave, the mountain falling away below them. The lights from the houses in the valley below were pinpoints, like stars in the sky. He swooped closer and she saw the people moving about, going about their routine of modern life. She saw the cars, the fenced yards and the power lines that Brian had tried to explain to her.

"This world is not part of your own, Spirit Singer. You are from the Old Way, and the bridge between the old and this new one is

through the man-child, Brian. His spirit is now living in both worlds. Teach him, and let him teach you. This world that he is part of will soon change forever. The ways of your people will once again make the difference between living and dying," Puma said to her as he carried them far above the dwindling landscape, spiraling up, up into the night sky.

"Now look, look down at the world as it is, and soon not to be."

She could see the lights of a thousand cities below. The immensity of the new civilization overwhelmed her. They descended toward a large metropolitan city with skyscrapers and multi-level expressways. Here, the hustle and bustle of life did not end at dusk.

The streets and sidewalks teemed with cars and people. Light from the thousands of neon signs, streetlights and buildings illuminated the night sky for hundreds of feet above the city.

Keechie had no idea of the sheer size of the world, and even less of the vastness of the modern ways of humanity. She realized at once how much the people depended on their new technology and modern ways, and how unprepared they would be without them. She also realized that she had no place in this new world, but she was comforted by that thought instead of being saddened by it.

They circled the mountain that she knew so well, and descended towards the familiar cave and the only home that she had ever known. A feeling of comfort and security came over her.

She opened her eyes and saw she was once again in front of the fireplace, and felt the comfort of her sleeping furs beneath her. She snuggled into them, hugged Granny Boo's Power Bundle to her chest, and immediately went to sleep with a peaceful smile on her face.

Chapter Thirteen
"Dad, Meet Keechie"

It was Sunday, and Dad and I were in the back yard finishing up a new rock and concrete smoker oven. It was beginning to look like an igloo to me. We lined it with almost pure kaolin clay, which we would fire slowly, until vitrified into a non-porous surface. If it worked as planned, it would be a smoker, an oven and a grill. All we had left to do was to fire the clay, then fit the door.

"Your mom's been telling me about your new friend, Brian," Dad commented as he began shoveling the hot coals into the new oven.

"She sounds like an interesting woman. So she's mostly Indian, huh?"

"Yep, her mother was pure Creek Indian, and her father was half Indian and half black. He was from Louisiana—probably Creole. That makes Keechie three-quarters Indian, the way I figure it."

"Sounds about right to me... why don't you bring her back next weekend? I knew an old Indian man once. He was in the Philippines with me in World War Two—in the army. He was one of those

Navajo Indians that they used to send top secret radio messages in their language. The Japs couldn't understand a word they said. Helped us win the war!"

I tried not to let the surprise show on my face. I knew Dad didn't hate blacks, but I also knew how he felt about having black guests in his home. It was ingrained into his generation, inherited from parents, grandparents and community. It would take generations to eliminate from the mindset of a nation just barely free from the horrors of slavery.

"Thanks, Dad. I'll go get her next Sunday morning. Maybe we can have Grandma over too. They're about the same age, and both know a lot about herbs and stuff. Maybe this new smoker will be ready by then too. We could fire it up Saturday night and smoke a big pork roast all night."

We added more coals to the new fire pit, and covered the whole thing, except for the chimney, with wet burlap bags. Later we would build the fire up hotter and hotter, until the kaolin cured completely.

The first week of school went slowly. I was anxious for the weekend visit, and on Wednesday after school, I went to the cave to invite Keechie to the Sunday barbecue.

I parked at the Rock, and was almost to the burial ground when she spoke.

"Been 'spectin' ya, Brine. Knowed you wuz busy wit' school n' all."

"Were you waiting on me, Keechie? How did you know I was coming today?"

"Hee, hee, Brine. I juss knowed ya wuz a'comin' back. I wuz juss vistin' m' fokes and checkin' on everthang. Collectin' some fresh herbs an' stuff. Enjoyin' da weather befo' hit get too cole."

I told her about the weekend, and my dad's interest in meeting her.

"My grandma will be there too, Keechie. The two of you have a lot in common. It'll be fun, and we're having pork. It'll be a change from venison for both of us!"

Keechie wondered if she should tell Brian about Puma Man yet, or if she should tell him at all. She was still trying to absorb the message from her vision the night before, and had already decided to wait for the appropriate time to tell him.

But to juss mention my visits t' da spirit world couldn't hurt, she thought.

" 'Member dat dream ya had las' week, Brine? De one 'bout callin' da animals? I has dose kinda dreams alla time, only dey's differnt from dreams. Dey's mo lak spiritwalkin', Granny Boo call it."

"I know what she means, Keechie. They are sure different. Sometimes I feel like I'm wide awake when they happen. Sometimes there is this... this man... with a cat face... more like a leopard or cougar or something. Could he be the same one I saw while I was holding your Grandad's spear?"

"Puma!" she blurted out. "Hit's Puma man. Least dat's whut Granny Boo called 'im," she added with a thoughtful look on her face.

Dass whut Puma was a'talkin' bout las' night. He already been a'workin' on Brine all dis time. Sometime he mo' lak Fox wit' all 'is tricks.

"Puma Man?" I asked, surprised at her answer. "You have seen him too, Keechie?"

"Yep, he kinda my totem—my spirit guide. He been part of m' tribe since Granny Boo kin 'member, an' 'er Granny befo' 'er. Dat's how come 'er Clan wuz de Puma Clan. He show you thangs you ain't nevva thought 'bout, Brine. He came t' me las' night and tole me you wuz ready t' learn 'bout da spirit worl'. He say you the bridge 'tween the old worl' an' dis new 'un."

She hoped this wasn't too much information, or too soon, but Puma had spoken.

"He was there when we buried your dad and brother, wasn't he? I felt him then, while you were playing the drum and singing."

"Yep, he were dere alright. Him and some others too. I wondered iffen ya seen dem."

We spent the rest of the afternoon talking and collecting herbs and roots. Keechie described them and their uses as we worked. She showed me how to spot them in different seasons, and how each was prepared for their different uses.

It was almost dark when we parted, and I could feel her watching me as I climbed back up to where I had parked my car.

Early Sunday morning, I went to get my grandma and took her to my house. She and Mom could work together in the kitchen getting everything else ready that went with the barbecue. Mom could also prepare Grandma for meeting Keechie before she got there. Since she had grown up as a girl in a house without electricity and was the same age, she wouldn't need all that much preparation.

Keechie was waiting for me at the rock again, excited about the visit and another ride in the car. This time she climbed in without fear. She was wearing another of the dresses I had bought her and had a beautiful silver and turquoise clasp in her hair. She also wore the elegant squash blossom necklace that had belonged to her Granny Boo.

"Wait 'til you see the new smoker oven dad and I made, Keechie. It worked great. That pork roast was falling apart this morning when we checked on it," I told her as we pulled into the driveway.

Everyone was waiting on the porch for us when we got out of the car. Mom was first to greet Keechie and gave her a hug, which Keechie accepted, looking hesitant at first. She then led her to Grandma.

"Mama, this is Keechie, our new friend."

Grandma took both of her hands and greeted her warmly.

"Call me Irma, Keechie. I'm glad to meet you."

"And this is my dad, Keechie. His name is Brian too. I was named after him."

Keechie appeared somewhat unsure of herself, but approached him and offered her hand.

Dad took it and said, "Welcome, Keechie. Brian told me a lot about you, but he didn't tell me you were so young!"

"Hee, hee, Mista Brine. Brine din' tell me ya wuz so young either... an' hansome too!"

We all laughed, mostly in relief, as we walked into the house. Keechie and dad had both handled the situation well. It was going to be a wonderful day.

Dad and I brought the roast in and began slicing and shredding it up while the women talked and worked in the kitchen. They were making coleslaw, potato salad, and brunswick stew, with sweet pickles, potato chips and sesame seeded buns to go along with the pork. Keechie had never seen most of these things, and was amazed at the volume and variety of food. She was fascinated with the old manual food grinder that Mom was using to make the slaw. She asked if she could "tarn de hannel." Then she took over the whole process. She was like a kid with a new toy, and soon we had more slaw than we could eat in a week!

No one said a word when we began eating and Keechie pulled out the knife I had given her. She watched us as we ate and tried very hard to do everything the same, except for using her own knife on the pork. Occasionally she would forget and stab a piece with the knife and use it in place of a fork, but she did it daintily and with dignity.

After dinner, Mom cleared the table and we all sat and talked. Dad was more interested in Keechie's survival skills than the talk of food, and they talked at length about getting by without stores and modern conveniences.

Then Mom ran us "menfolk" out of the kitchen so she, Grandma and Keechie could talk. Every time Dad or I would go back to get a refill of tea, or another beer for Dad, they would pause in their conversation until we left.

"Don't let it worry you, boy. Women just do that. They could be talking about laundry and will do the same thing. You know, Keechie sure sounds like a ni... a black person talking, but she sure is smart about survival stuff. She would be one to have around if you ever had to live off the land. She told me she could start a fire without matches. Did you know that? I know how, but I never have been able to do it!"

I heard his near racial slur, but appreciated his catching it in time. It was a sign he was trying, and that he thought of Keechie with respect.

"Yep, Dad, I knew she could do it, but she usually has coals left over in her fireplace. She plans it that way."

Mom and Grandma made Keechie a "to-go" bag of pork and all the trimmings to take home. This was a typical thing to do, and Keechie appreciated the gesture. Mom also made her up a sack full of store-bought spices and several jars of jelly, pickles and relish that she and grandma put up during the summer. Keechie liked the pickles especially. She had kept going back for more. Vinegar was one thing she had never had access to.

Unknown to Keechie, Mom had also placed the old food grinder and several different sized head attachments in the bag. It would be a much appreciated surprise gift when she found it.

They all went to the car with us, gave Keechie a warm farewell and invited her back.

"Come back anytime," Dad told her as he put his arm around her shoulders and gave them a squeeze.

"I enjoyed your visit, Keechie—and call me Brian. Never did feel like a mister, especially to my elders," he said with a smile. He had really enjoyed her visit, and sounded sincere.

As we made our way back up the mountain, Keechie asked me to play the radio for her again. I found a station that was playing "Big Band" music. She didn't have a clue to what the instruments were, but kept perfect time with her feet on the floorboard.

I promised her another visit next weekend before she made her way down the rocks. She turned and waved as I stood watching her go, very aware of the love I felt for her—the same love that I felt for my immediate family. She was very much a part of that family now— more so than I would know for many years.

Chapter Fourteen
Planning for the Future

Ever since I picked up my first arrowhead, I knew I wanted to be an archaeologist. There was a feeling of connecting with the previous owner when I touched these ancient relics. Images and scenes of past civilizations that seemed more like memories than imagination would flood my brain. I began studying everything I could find on Native American culture, especially those of the southeastern United States. By the time I met Keechie, I had expanded my studies to include all the indigenous cultures around the world.

My dad just didn't understand.

"Who's gonna pay you to dig in the dirt?" he asked me on more than one occasion. "Better get you a job that you get paid for."

As I tried to prepare myself for college during my next two years of high school, I was torn between following his advice, or my real desire to be an archeologist. The cost of a college education was out of my dad's reach, and I knew that I must "work my way" through college. I was resigned to that fact, but I didn't want to waste an education on something that I couldn't get paid for either.

The answer came from an unexpected source.

The old coins and bills saved by Keechie's father were more valuable than I had ever imagined. My friend in LaGrange had shown them to his father, who had appraised them. It seemed that several of the gold coins were very rare. Many of the other coins were scarce and in great demand by collectors. I had only given him samples of the different coins, and by calculating the value of these and multiplying by the number that I actually had, the entire value came to over one hundred and fifty thousand dollars. That didn't include the duplicates that I had set aside for my own collection!

He had returned all the samples I had given him, along with a report of their values. I stashed them away in my closet. They were just too valuable for me to consider them mine. Keechie must be told and given the choice of changing her life completely. She could now buy a house and enter modern society. Somehow, I knew what her answer would be, but I had to give her the choice.

I had two more years of high school before selecting a college, but it was time to begin focussing my classes toward the right curriculum.

The University of Georgia in Athens offered the degree I wanted, but I had always been drawn to Texas A&M. The out-of-state fees had placed that choice out of my range. Now, with the help of George Washington, it became a real possibility. Also, my grades were good enough so far to qualify for a modest scholarship —that is, if I could maintain them for the next two years.

Almost every weekend during those last two years I was with Keechie. Frequently I took my homework to the Rock, and she sat with me and watched silently as I completed the assignments. She especially enjoyed American History. I would read aloud and she asked very intelligent questions, which caused me to retain more of what I was reading.

During a chapter on the Native Americans of the Southwest, she recognized the cultural traditions as being the same as those of her tribe.

"Dose prolly my tribe, befo' somma dem come hyer," she commented as she studied the pictures of the artifacts.

"Granny Boo could tell what dose marks mean on dose pots an' blankets. I knows somma dem."

One day, near the end of my senior year, as we finished up a particularly long assignment and were enjoying the sunset, I told her about the value of her father's money.

"You could buy a house in the valley, Keechie. You could have a refrigerator and television. You could have friends and go to the store for everything you need."

"Brine, my Pap wanted t' send us kids to school wit' dat money. Hit too late fer dat, and I already gots everthang I needs. Vistin' yo fokes ever once in a while is all I needs fer compny."

"It's just so much money, Keechie. I feel selfish by taking it."

"Dat money be yores t' go t' school. You da one meant fer Pap's money. Puma done tol' me so. He say you gonna make a differnce in dis worl'. You and de fambly you gone ta have."

Then she said something so prophetic that the words bored into my soul, but would not be proven true until nearly forty years later.

"You's gone ta have a girl chil' wit' da Gift, same as me an' Granny Boo. Puma done tole me dat too. She gonna make a differnce in dis worl'."

We sat staring at each other for a long moment. The seriousness and resolve in her expression told me that no words in response were necessary. I put my arm around her shoulders and drew her to me. We sat there with her head on my shoulder as the sky changed into a beautiful magenta and red kaleidoscope, and the valley below us disappeared into the shadow of the mountain.

It was the first time she had allowed that much physical contact.

Chapter Fifteen
Graduation

The Harris County High School auditorium was packed on graduation night, May 15th, 1961. I was sitting on stage between my two best friends who had been with me for the entire twelve years. Neither of them had ever met Keechie, but they both knew of her.

"Is that her, Brian?" Jimmy asked, pointing toward my parents and the diminutive woman sitting between them.

"Yep, that's her. I asked her to wear that dress tonight, and the jewelry," I replied. "She made that dress herself, and the jewelry was her Grandma's. It's probably two hundred years old, and came from her tribe when they were still in the Southwest. I think it's either Navajo or Zuni."

Luanne asked, "Why didn't you ever bring her around to meet us? She seems so interesting... I really would like to get to know her."

"She is just getting used to being around people, Luanne. She has been living all alone for over fifty years! I didn't want to rush her into society all at once."

Keechie had been reluctant to come at the last minute, but my parents had insisted.

"You have been an inspiration to Brian, Keechie. You are special to him and to us," my mom told her as we prepared to leave.

"You have become a member of our family. Brian will be disappointed if you don't come, okay?"

"I'se juss be skeered of all dose people," Keechie said. "I'se goin', but I sho don' know how t' be 'roun' people."

"You just sit there and be yourself, Keechie," my dad told her. "You can sit between us, and be there for Brian."

My dad had come to really like the woman, and had even asked me to bring her back to visit more than once during the past two years. He treated her more like his mother who died several years before. He never once mentioned her racial heritage. That was a milestone for him.

Keechie was lovely, and even though she was dressed in her full Indian attire, did not look out of place. We made eye contact and I gave her a wave and a smile. She waved back and then looked around to see if anyone had noticed. She looked back at me, beaming with pride and smiling.

After the ceremonies ended, and we rejoined our parents and families, it seemed that everyone wanted to meet Keechie. They were fascinated with her —for both her Indian origins and her association with me. I introduced her as part of my extended family and tried to make her feel comfortable with all the attention she was receiving.

Most of my class were going to a graduation party afterwards, but I had begged off. I wanted this night with my family and Keechie. Dad had made reservations at a very exclusive restaurant on the bank of the Chattahoochee River near Columbus, Georgia. They specialized in "All-You-Can-Eat" catfish with all the trimmings, and served it in private dining rooms, overlooking the river. Keechie was ecstatic, and became the center of attention among my family members who had not met her.

After dinner, the graduation gifts were brought out and I was having a great time opening them. When the last one was opened and all the gift-wrapping cleaned up, Keechie drew me aside.

"Dey be one mo giff fer ya, Brine. Hit's not wrapped up, but yo Mam hepped me wit' it, fer da size an' all."

Dad came in at that moment carrying her gift. It was a complete buckskin outfit, pants and shirt, of the softest leather you could imagine. It was modestly decorated with beadwork and quilled patterns. A pair of beautiful moccasins completed the set.

"Hit's from the two deers you kilt dat day wit' da bow an' arrow, Brine. Hopes ya lak it."

It was a work of art. It was completely original and made by loving, talented hands. The stitching and decorations were immaculately precise. My mom and grandma both admired and commented on the talent that was so apparent in the design.

Keechie spent that night with us in the guest bedroom. The next morning when I went to wake her, she wasn't in the bed. She was in the floor with a couple of blankets.

"Dat bed wuz a'swallerin' me," she said grumpily, with more than a hint of humor.

"Hit's so soff hit kep' me 'wake."

Since it was Saturday, Dad was getting ready for work and Mom was fixing breakfast for us. Keechie wanted to help but Mom wouldn't let her.

"You just let me make breakfast for you, Keechie. You are the guest of honor."

Instead of taking Keechie back to her cave right away, I first took her to my dad's store. When we walked in, she stopped and looked around with an awed expression on her face.

"Dis be da same sto my Pap took me when I wuz a l'il girl! Hit ain't changed much since den. I usta stan' right over dere nex' to dat old stove an' jus' smell all da smells."

My dad had worked in this store since the end of the World War II, and had only recently bought it from the original owner who had hired him. It had been in his family for at least two generations, and had not changed much in the interim.

"Where da canny, Brine? I wants me some canny real bad!"

Dad laughed and handed her a large paper bag.

"Fill it up, Keechie. Your dad's credit is still good here!"

Most of that summer I worked as a surveyor's assistant. Our neighbor, the county surveyor, was a graduate of the University of Georgia, and had recommended that I look into beginning my studies there. He had a degree in horticulture, and was an avid outdoorsman. Most of our work that summer was what he called "deep woods" projects, and it took us all over the state.

Since creeks and rivers were often used as property boundary lines, we frequently found ourselves in the middle of ancient Indian village sites. He would carefully record the site and then... work would cease!

We spent many entire days on our hands and knees searching for potsherds and arrowheads, and the amazing thing was that I was getting paid for it!

Dad's question, "Who's gonna pay you to dig in the dirt?" was answered!

Through some of his alumni contacts, he began the process of arranging a scholarship for me at his Alma Mater, and I was accepted into the Anthropology program. This would be a good start for me, and it was much closer to home, family and Keechie. I made my plans to spend at least two years there, and finish up at Texas A&M.

Chapter Sixteen
Another Graduation, and a Surprise

Keechie and my family became even closer while I was away at college. She, my mom and grandma would get together and swap stories and herbal remedies. Keechie shared her knowledge of wild plants and herbs with them and they taught her how to knit and crochet. Dad kept her well stocked with supplies from the "Sto", and Keechie repaid him with her skill in skinning rabbits!

He had begun raising rabbits as a hobby several years before, and built several hutches in our barnyard. At one time, he had over five hundred rabbits, for which he kept immaculate records. He had the Food Inspector certify the rabbits for consumption so he could sell fresh dressed rabbits from his store.

The part he had the most problem with was on slaughter day. He would skin and dress one rabbit while Keechie would do five, and her method left the hides usable. He didn't want the hides, so Keechie took them and prepared them.

The day came when she said, "I gots mo rabbit hides than I gonna evva need. Oughtta be sumpin we could do wit' 'em 'stead a wastin' 'em."

That gave Dad the idea of turning the furs into a profitable venture. Our neighbor, J.D. Moye, a trapper among many other talents, made a decent living selling mink, fox, beaver and rabbit hides. Dad asked him if he would add the rabbit pelts to his stock for half of the profit. J.D. agreed, and when the sales were made, Dad offered Keechie the money.

"Don' need no money. Juss put it towards the stuff you brangs me from da sto."

His respect for the woman must have doubled at that moment!

During my two years at the University of Georgia, I could get home for a weekend about twice a month. Texas A&M in College Station, Texas was a different story. I was lucky to get home once in every three months.

I missed my family and Keechie terribly during those years, but it was then that I began writing my story about Keechie. It began as a small journal, but the more homesick I became, the more I would write.

I told some of her story to one of my instructors in a Cultural Anthropology class, and he became very interested. When I showed him my journal, he offered even more encouragement,

"A classic example of cross-cultural integration, Brian. This is term paper material!"

And that's what it became. I wrote my thesis titled *The Muskogee Indian Nation of the Southeast*, which included the Upper, Middle and Lower Creek tribes. I researched their origins, migration routes, their culture and their final plight dealing with the influx of the Spanish, and later the Europeans, into their homelands. I wrote of the many broken treaties by the United States government, and of the Indians' final removal to the reservations of what is now Oklahoma.

The story of Keechie and her ancestors who refused to leave and thrived in a cave in Pine Mountain, Georgia was woven throughout the thesis. It was a story of determination, resolve and survival in a world dominated by white men and the modern world. Thanks to Keechie,

I received the highest marks possible on the paper.

On graduation night, I expected to see my parents there. They were to drive the nearly one thousand miles to watch me graduate. When they arrived on the afternoon of the Big Event, I met them outside my dormitory, and as I was hugging and greeting them, saw movement over my mom's shoulder from the back seat of the car. It was a smiling, little woman that was such an inspirational part of my life.

"Hee,hee, Brine, I sho is glad t' be hyer. I done hat me 'nuff ca ridin' t' lass me a while! Yo daddy tol' me dat the sojers made my people walk all dis fa when dey leff da mountin!"

I could hardly believe it! This would make my graduation complete, just as it had when I finished high school. I had wanted all my friends here to meet Keechie, especially the professor who caused me to write my term paper on her people.

On the stage that night, as I waited for my name to be called for my diploma, I looked out into the audience for my parents and Keechie. At my request, she was wearing her traditional Indian outfit and looking as elegant as ever. I waved at her just as I had during my high school graduation, and she waved back.

The professor, who had read my journal and advised me to make it my thesis, was on stage near me and noticed the exchange. He made eye contact with me with a questioning look on his face, and I nodded in agreement.

Yep, that's her. The one who made all this possible with her inspiration, her father's money and her spirit guide, Puma Man.

After the ceremony I made a beeline for them. I hugged my parents, then removed my cap and placed it on Keechie's head.

"You earned this as much as I did," I told her as I embraced her tiny body.

My mentor, the professor of Cultural Anthropology, followed me to them. He took Keechie's hands in his and spoke to her in a strange language.

She looked shocked at first, then spoke back, apparently in the same language. He laughed and gave her a warm embrace.

He turned to my parents and I and said sheepishly, "I tried to say in Muskogean, 'You honor us with your presence, Grandmother'."

"An' I set I ain't no Granny, but iffen I wuz, I would call Brine my grandson. Hee, hee, I ain't heerd dat talk since my Mam died. Pap din' 'low us t' talk no Injun."

We all laughed and then introduced Keechie around the circle of staff and students who wanted to meet her. She was suddenly the center of attention, and if she was ever going to get over her fear of being around people, this was her chance!

Chapter Seventeen
Keechie's Reunion

I had another surprise in store for Keechie. During my research on the Muskogee and Creek nations, I located the reservation in central Oklahoma where the members of her tribe had been re-located – at least those that had survived the journey. Many died along the way from starvation, disease and most likely, broken hearts. There was just a possibility that some of her ancestor's relatives still remained on the reservation, but at the very least, she could again be among her people.

My old 1952 Chevrolet was traded for a newer 1956 model. It stood a better chance of making the trip to College Station, Texas two years earlier, so as my parents left to return to Georgia, Keechie and I struck out almost due north for the reservations of Oklahoma.

If you expected to see teepees and totem poles, The reservation was nothing like you would imagine. It looked more like a huge, lower class, suburban housing project placed in a desert. The main part of town consisted of a few shops that sold "Genuine Indian Crafts" and the like to tourists. There were a couple of service stations and general stores and that was about it. In general, the inhabitants ignored us.

"How are we ever going to find your people, Keechie? Who should we begin asking for anyone who would remember your tribe?"

"I gots me an idee, Brine. Let's go to dat sto ova dere dat sell Injun stuff," she said as we walked around the sleepy little town square.

A bell tinkled on the door as the two of us walked into the small shop.

"Hep ya?" a middle-aged Indian woman asked, not even looking up at us.

"Do you got any drums?" Keechie asked her, then repeated the same question in the Creek dialect.

With that, the woman looked up at Keechie with surprise, but then said, "I got a few drums, but I never did learn no Injun talk. Look right over there on that bottom shelf. That's all I got," she said, pointing behind us.

Keechie went to the shelf and thumped a few of the "handmade" drums.

"Dis 'un'll do," she said as she thumped the last one.

"How 'bout rattles?"

"Top shelf," the woman sighed in obvious boredom.

The handmade Indian items with "Made in Taiwan" stickers cost nearly fifteen dollars, but when Keechie had an idea, it was usually worth paying for.

"We needs t' change clothes, Brine. You gots t' hep me wit dis. Did you brang dat deerhide suit I made ya?" she asked with growing excitement.

"I sure did, Keechie. It's in my suitcase. I wore it a lot this past winter! It's the warmest thing I had to wear. We passed a motel just before we got into town, so let's go back there and get us a room. I have a feeling we will be staying here a few days."

We rented a room with two double beds in the nearly deserted motel. The clerk never looked up at us. I had no idea what Keechie was planning, but this was getting interesting. She was anxious to get back into town, so after a short rest, and playing with the controls on the rattly air conditioner, we changed into our "Indian Outfits" and headed back into town.

I parked on the town square just before sundown, and she removed the drum and rattle from the back seat.

"Let's go ova dere to dat l'il hill in da middle o' dis place. You sees den whut I'se gonna do. Hee, hee."

No one noticed us as we climbed the small hill. There were only a few locals and a few more tourists in sight as Keechie handed me the rattle.

" 'Memba when ya hepped me burr m' Pap an' m' brother?" she asked, as she took the drum and began a slow cadence beat upon it.

I sat with my back against the one little tree there and shook the rattle in time with her drumming as I had done with her before.

After a few minutes, Keechie seemed to go into a kind of trance. With her eyes closed and face raised to the sky, she began singing. It was the "Come To Me" song I had heard the old woman singing in my dream.

I took my free hand and reached beneath my shirt for the medicine bag that she had given me over four years ago. A surge of energy came from it that carried me to another reality that existed somehow in this same time and place

Although she was singing softly, it seemed that her voice was echoing through the entire town. Waves of energy pulsated from her voice and I felt the presence of another dimension shimmering through my mind.

Then I saw the Puma Man appear above us, covering the entire sky.

People stopped in their tracks, then began gathering at the foot of the hill. No one spoke. All other sounds from the town had ceased. Even the shop owners left their businesses and came to the square.

It was a surrealistic scene developing before us as the Song continued. The people began swaying to the tempo, but Keechie seemed oblivious to them, and continued the enchanted drumming and singing.

Somehow I found myself standing beside her and blending my voice with hers as I felt the power of Puma Man overtake my spirit. I used no words, but chanted in harmony with the Song. My very soul was singing. Then the words began coming out of my mouth. I had no idea of their meaning, but they were the same words that Keechie was singing.

Keechie increased the tempo faster and faster until I could barely keep up, then with a staccato flourish on the drum, and a final sizzle of the rattle we ended the Song.

There was total silence among the crowd. She spoke something in her native language then gazed out among the people with her arms raised to the sky.

One old man, who had never once taken his eyes from Keechie, slowly came forward to the base of the hill. He spoke to her briefly in the same tongue, then switched to English.

"Sister, I have not heard that song since I was a little boy. My grandmother was a Singer and a Healer among my people. She sang that song that called the animals. Several of her grandchildren have learned the words, but no one has ever sang it like that!"

The crowd had begun breaking up and going back to their routines as if it had been just a show for tourists. In a few moments, there was only this one old man left with us.

"Whar yo people come from?" Keechie asked him.

"I was born here on this reservation, Spirit Singer, but my grandmother's grandmother came here from Georgia, from a mountain across the Chattahoochee River. They walked all the way here. She was a Chief's daughter. 'Old Bull Killer', she called him. She told us the stories of him many times—of how he earned his name, and of how he died refusing to leave his mountain. His wife's mother, Willow, was one of the most powerful medicine woman in the whole Muskogee nation, she told us."

Keechie looked at me questioningly.

"If his granny's granny were Bull Killer's daughter, den she be Granny Boo's kin?"

"Seems that way to me, Keechie. I believe you have found your family."

She handed me the drum, then extended her hands to the old man.

"Bull Killer was my Granny's grandfather's father," she told him as they held hands in greeting. They stood that way for a long moment, just looking at each other. Then they exchanged some words in the old language, and both smiled as if they had shared a private joke.

Keechie looked at me and said, "He say dat dey all thought dat dey wuz de onliest ones leff from our tribe."

"I jess tol' him same as I done tol' you. 'As long as dey's someone who kin hyer da drums, da People will never die'. Dat sayin' goes all de way back to Wild Dancer, de one who furs' come t' de valley."

We sat down beneath the small tree in the square, and the two cousins who had been born half a nation apart became acquainted.

As he sat facing her, he said, "My great grandmother told my grandmother that she had left a younger sister there, along with a few others. She thought the soldiers had killed them all. My mother never learned the Singing, but my younger sister is the Medicine Woman and Healer here. She told me that only every other generation had the Gift, but there are only a few here that hold to the old ways."

Keechie had remained silent the whole time he had been talking, but now spoke up.

"De ol' ways were all I evva knowed. I din' have no choice dere!"

Will you be staying here a while? You must meet the rest of your family!"

"I sho ain't gonna leave widout meetin' my fambly. We gots t' stay long 'nuff fer dat."

She thought for a moment, then asked the man, "Was your Granny's name Cornsilk? Granny Boo always say dat her granny's big sister Cornsilk hat leff wit' her fambly an' da others. She say

Cornsilk was a Healer more'n her granny..."

"Yes! Yes it was! My Indian name is Long Walker, by the way, but they call me William here. Where did you get the name, 'Keechie'?"

"Hit be fer Kachina, but why dey call you Long Walker?"

"It was because when I was a little boy, I would walk away from the settlement. Once they hunted me for two days and nights. I always wanted to go to where my grandmother and mother came from, across the Chattahoochee River. The place she told me about that she left always seemed so much better than here."

"I sho do wanna meet de fambly an' 'spechully yo sister, Long Walker. We's got us some ketchin' up t' do!"

They continued talking until well past dark, and when we were about to leave, they made plans to meet here the next day. They embraced each other and said goodbye in their old language.

At the motel room that night, Keechie seemed agitated. She couldn't sit still and kept pacing the room.

"What's wrong, Keechie?"

"Evathang's fine, Brine. Hit's juss dat I keeps a'thankin' 'bout my beautiful place I stays at, all alone, and dis awful place whar all my kin came to. Hit juss ain't fair to none o' us. I sho wooden' wanna live hyer, but I done missed out on my whole fambly bein' tagedder. Watchin' da kids grow up an' all. Jus' bein' happy t' fin' dem agin make me sad at da same time! I'se all confused 'bout whut I feel inside."

"Well, tomorrow you get to meet some of your family, Keechie. You can learn of the family you missed. Maybe you'll feel better then. Would you like to be alone for a little while?"

"No, Brine, been 'lone too much as 'tis. But I sho would lak to go outside fer a while. Let's go look at da sky an' feel da wind."

The western sky was still glowing with the recent sunset. Magenta and purple clouds filled our view as we lay there on our backs on the ground. We didn't speak, but I could feel Mother

Earth's healing energy flow through me. I Looked over at Keechie, and it was apparent that she was feeling the same.

I reached out and took her hand as we lay there until darkness overtook us. It became too cold to enjoy the peacefulness, so we went back inside and almost instantly went to sleep—me on one of the beds, and Keechie on a pallet in the floor next to the other one.

Long Walker was waiting on us when we pulled up to the town square.

"My aunt and sister are waiting to meet you, Keechie. They were so excited last night when I told them about you. They scolded me for not bringing you home right then!"

He hopped into the back seat and gave directions to his house.

It was a large wood-framed ranch home several miles from the town proper. There were a few small trees and a flower garden in the front yard with potted plants hanging on the porch.

As soon as we got out of the car, two women rushed to meet us. The older woman looked so much like Keechie that the kinship was immediately apparent.

The younger woman, Long Walker's sister, spoke first.

"Welcome to our home, Kachina. This is our aunt, Moonflower. She is our mother's youngest sister. She is nearly one hundred years old. Speak loudly, for she does not hear very well; and I am Pumawoman. What a name for a girl, huh?" she said with a hint of sarcasm in her voice, but exchanged a knowing look with Keechie. The reference to Puma was not lost on me.

They were immediately like any other family anywhere in the world. Everyone was talking at once and laughing and doing that thing that only women can do—keep up with several conversations at once. Long Walker and I were left standing there open-mouthed, trying to keep up with the flow of words.

Then Keechie introduced me,

"An' dis hyer be Brine. He be da one who foun' out 'bout y'all an' brung me hyer. He lak a son t' me. He gots da Gift, only he don' know it yet."

We all went inside where a huge breakfast had been prepared. The women continued their spirited conversation while we ate. Soon other family members began showing up. They were all anxious to meet this relative of theirs that had remained in Georgia. They wanted to hear the stories of the others that remained in spite of the government's demand that they leave.

Keechie was ecstatic over having a family at last, and was as happy as I had ever seen her. It made no difference that some of the relatives came from the paternal side of the family. They were all family, and that was what mattered most.

Moonflower suddenly lifted her ancient body from her chair and raised her hand. The room fell silent.

"We are blessed this day with the presence of our long-lost sister. She is the granddaughter of our grandmother's sister, both daughters of the great mico, Bull Killer. She, like our Pumawoman here, has the Gift. I am calling for a special council of our tribal elders. There will be a festival in her honor. Not just our family, but everyone, should share in this news. Everyone here comes from families who were driven from their ancestral homes and brought here."

"I've never heard her say that many words at once in my whole life," Long Walker said to me in a whisper, and then laughed.

"She will get her way too. She IS one of the tribal council and one of the most respected. She holds to the old ways, speaks the old language fluently, and even though she wasn't of the 'every other generation' of those who received the Gift, has acquired it through sheer determination and dedication to preserving our spiritual culture. Puma Man has become your totem also, I gather?"

"I think so. He appeared to me again yesterday while Keechie and I were doing the Song. I saw him for the first time in a dream just after meeting Keechie, and she gave me this," I told him as I pulled the medicine bag from beneath my shirt.

"She said it was Granny Boo's. I've never taken it off since."

He started to touch it but hesitated. "It is a special gift, Brian. It contains the memories of a people that will never die as long as there are those who remember. Pass it on to your children and their children. Tell them the story of Kachina and her people. Tell them of the Puma Man. Some will understand, some will not, but as long as there is just one…," he said with emotion filling his voice just as another group of family members arrived and joined the spontaneous reunion.

Chapter Eighteen
The Council Meeting

The Council of Elders met the following evening, with Keechie as the special guest of honor. She was perturbed because I would not be going in with her, but I was neither of Indian descent nor a member of the tribe.

"You'll be fine, Keechie. I will be right outside with the others, waiting for you. You are the Guest of Honor, and I am very proud of you," I told her as the members began filing inside. She gave me a quick, self-conscious hug and walked in with her head high, not showing any of the reluctance I knew she felt.

I realized that the hug I had just received was the first I had ever received from Keechie that she had initiated! Something else was strange. Ever since we had left the motel room she had been carrying a small cloth-wrapped package, and she was still clutching it tightly as the door closed behind her.

An hour passed, then two, and those of us waiting outside were growing restless when Long Walker came to the door.

"They want you inside, Brian," he said with a smile.

Now I was as nervous as Keechie had been. What could they possibly want with me?

"Welcome, young Brian," Moonflower greeted me from the head of the long council table.

"You are the author of this manuscript?"

She passed me a very familiar manilla folder.

So that's what Keechie had been carrying. It was my college thesis on the Muskogee Indians!

"Yes Ma'am. This is my term paper that I wrote in college," I replied hesitantly, wondering if it had somehow offended the council or the Indian Nation as a whole.

"Kachina told me about it yesterday and I asked her to bring it with her tonight. We have read most of it aloud to the Council. We sincerely hope we have not offended you by doing so?" Moonflower made the last statement into a question.

"No, Ma'am, not at all. I was hoping that I had not offended your people by something I wrote in it."

Since Keechie could not read I had read her bits of its contents, and had given her credit for inspiring me to write it. Since then she had treated it like an icon and held it like a holy object.

"Quite the contrary, young man," said the man sitting at the end of the table opposite Moonflower. "Your term paper is well-researched and factual, but that's not what impressed us the most. It was your heart-feeling your manuscript conveyed within the stories of your friend, Kachina, and of her people, your desire to learn of the Indian way of life, and especially your visions of the Puma Man. He has accepted you as a member of this tribe, and we, the Muskogee Nation, would be remiss if we did not do the same."

Keechie rose and stood by my side as I stood there in astonishment.

She whispered in my ear, "He da big mico here, Brine. He be da chief!"

The entire council stood and applauded their agreement as Moonflower placed a beautiful headband with a single eagle feather on my head.

"I am deeply honored, Imathla Thlako," I stammered, hoping my attempt at the Creek words for "Big Chief" was successful.

He took both my hands and smiled.

"Not the big chief, young Brian. I am Bearpaw, only the chief of council and the Osochi Clan; but I thank you for the compliment. That was very good use of our tongue. Long Walker told us of your part in the Song that he heard you and Kachina sing in the square. He said that you called the Puma Man down from the sky!"

"Would it be possible for us to have a copy of your manuscript? Our children should know the history of our people. You are quite the storyteller, young man. That is a highly honored position in our culture."

"I am honored, Mico. You may keep the original. I can have copies made if you want them."

They made a place for me at the table beside Keechie as Bearpaw resumed the meeting.

"So, it has been decided that the festival in Kachina's honor will be held during the Green Corn Festival. There will be many others coming here for that occasion, and they will all want to meet old Bull Killer's many times granddaughter. She, like our Pumawoman, is descended from Willow, the greatest Spirit Singer the Muskogee Nation has ever known. Willow was the mother of old Bull Killer's wife, and was a descendant of the mother family of the entire Muskogee Nation, the Wind family out of Central America. In olden times, all the chiefs were chosen from this Wind Clan."

With that, the council meeting ended. Everyone filed past Keechie and I, welcoming us. When we went outside, Bearpaw called for the attention of the large gathering there.

Taking Keechie's hand he said, "This is our sister, Kachina, who comes from our old home across the Chattahoochee River. She is

Spirit Singer and Medicine Woman and is the great granddaughter of our own Bull Killer.

Taking my hand, he continued, "And this is Brian, the newest member of our tribe. Kowakatcu, the Puma Man, has chosen him and led him to Kachina. The two of them have honored the bones of our ancestors with the Ghost Dance. Young Brian here was holding the spear of Bull Killer when Puma came to him the first time. We welcome them to our home!"

The cheering crowd of well wishers surrounded us. Long Walker handed us a drum and rattle and asked us to sing again as we had done in the town square. Keechie looked at Bearpaw for approval. He smiled and nodded his head is assent.

The gathered people formed a circle with the two of us in the center. Keechie began the soft, slow thrumming on the drum and the crowd became silent. As she began the Song, I joined in with the rattle.

Again her voice took on that quality of coming from everywhere at once. She wasn't singing loudly, but the Song itself seemed to reverberate within one's soul. I pressed the medicine bag to my chest and found myself chanting in harmony with her as I had done before.

Then there was another voice singing with us. Pumawoman had joined us in the clearing and was adding her voice to ours.

Her face was wet with tears as she sang the ancient Song with her cousin. Images appeared in my mind as I looked up into the night sky. Faces of the Old Ones who had gone before were looking down on their people, and seemed pleased.

There was a swirling spiral of energy flowing upward and outward above us as we reached the end of the Song. With the final crescendo of drum and rattle, I saw the smiling feline face of Puma Man again, covering the entire sky above us.

There was a reverent silence among the gathering as we finished; then after a moment, they began cheering and applauding wildly. Keechie was welcomed as "Grandmother" and "Spirit Singer", while I was being called "Brother", "Storyteller" and "Grandson" by the tribal members.

Almost two hours passed before Long Walker and Pumawoman pulled us aside, asking that we follow them home.

"This will go on all night without us," Long Walker said.

"Our people have been needing to be reminded of their roots and their heritage, and the two of you have given that to them this night. This will continue until dawn with or without you here. Join us at our home. You cannot stay at that motel any longer. We insist!"

We made our way to our cars and drove in a procession to their home. Bearpaw and several of the other council members followed, and as soon as we arrived at their home, they showed us to our rooms. The house was larger than it appeared from the outside, and they were used to having their extended families as frequent guests.

Pumawoman and Moonflower prepared a quick snack for everyone and we all sat around the living room talking and becoming acquainted. They all wanted to hear Keechie's story – not only from her, but also from me. They all had a good laugh when we told them the story of the deer that I had killed with bow and arrow, and how Keechie had surprised me by screaming from the woods with her knife in her hand.

Keechie, with a wide grin on her face said, "Hit were lak da old days my Granny Boo tol' me 'bout. Brine kilt dat deer wit' one arrow! Right through da heart! He made me feel lak an Injun fer sho dat day! Hee, hee."

Bearpaw had been looking at me intently the whole time, and finally drew me aside.

"How about you and I going to the motel and getting the rest of your belongings? I would like to talk with you alone for a bit, and besides, I need some air."

"Sure, Mico... errr... what should I call you? I don't want to offend."

"Call me Bearpaw, or grandfather, if you wish. It would honor me for you to call me that. We need to give you an Indian name while we're at it. After reading your wonderful journal, and hearing your stories, I think 'Yoholo' fits rather well. It means 'Good Speaker' in Muskogee."

"You honor me once again, Grandfather. I will try to live up to my new name."

Everyone congratulated me on my new name, and Moonflower stood and told the story of the Storyteller.

She looked at Keechie as she said, "Our grandfather, Bull Killer's son was a storyteller. His name was Yakita-Hasse. It meant 'Interpreter of the Sun'. In those days, the storyteller was almost as important as the chief. Sometimes even more so, because he held in his words the memory of the People. Before a storyteller died he would choose a young man who had a good memory and who enjoyed telling stories, and teach him the old stories and the history of the Clan. In this way, our tribal memories were passed from one generation to the next. The Storyteller was never allowed to go to war, for if he was killed, the history would be lost forever. Yokita-Hasse also entertained the tribe in bad times with his stories of the animals. He would act out their movements and take on their mannerisms. In this way we learned of the things in nature and how it all was related. He made the children laugh. They all loved him, and they remembered the stories."

"So you see, young Yoholo, 'Good Speaker' is the perfect name for you!" Bearpaw said.

Bearpaw told the others where we were going and led me to his car, which was not blocked by the other cars as mine was. He drove us slowly toward the motel on the outskirts of town.

"You seem to understand the spirit world of our culture, Yoholo. Puma Man chose you for some purpose. Nothing ever happens by chance. There is a purpose, a plan if you will, far greater than you or I could ever understand right now. I believe you already feel this too?"

"Even before I met Keechie, Grandfather... Bearpaw, I felt drawn to the Native Americans. I think I may have been an Indian in a previous life!" We both laughed and I added, "And remember, I was looking for arrowheads the day I met her."

"And what of your future? What are your plans, now that you have finished college?"

"I was going to take the summer off. I have considered going back to school later for my PhD in Cultural Anthropology, but I really have not decided yet. I want very badly to continue in the field. Do research. Dig in the dirt—that kind of thing..."

Just at that moment, we arrived at the motel. Bearpaw went into the room with me and we quickly gathered our belongings and put them in the back seat of his car. He drove to the office where I turned the key in to the clerk.

He still did not look up when he said, "Past noon. No refunds."

Bearpaw took a different route when we left. He said that he wanted to show me something. He drove to a high point that overlooked the town and parked in what appeared to be a picnic area. We got out and walked a short distance from the car.

"Compare this to the land where you and Keechie live. That was the place we once called our home, Yoholo," he said as he pointed out across the barren landscape where only a few lights from the town, and even fewer from houses were visible. "Yet we still survive as a people; but more and more of our young ones are leaving for the big cities with no idea of their culture or their heritage. Many of them are even ashamed of being Native American. You and Keechie could help us change that." He looked me squarely in the eyes as he spoke.

"What can we do, Grandfather? What are you saying?"

"I want you and Kachina to stay with us here this summer, and then as long as you will after that. We have an opening in our school for a teacher of History. I am on the school board as well," he said with a smile. "Teach our children of their heritage, and tell them the history of their people. Kachina can help Pumawoman with her duties. She teaches the crafts and the old ways of medicine to the young girls. There is a need for both of you here, and I believe Kachina needs to be among her people again as well."

I didn't know what to say. The only thing I had planned for the summer was a two-week field trip on a dig in New Mexico with the

Anthropology Department from school. If I could still do that...

"I will talk to Keechie, Grandfather. We will need to go home first, but my heart tells me this is a good thing; but you have just met me. How can you be so sure I am the right one for this?"

"When I read your paper, Yoholo, the Spirits of our ancestors awakened in me. They told me that you were their messenger. Puma Man led you here. What else could I do?"

He led me back to his car and we returned to the others.

Although it was getting late in the evening, everyone was still there. It seemed they had been swapping the family stories from the time of the forced evacuation from Georgia to this reservation. Keechie was in the middle of the story of she and I finding the bones of her father and brother in the deep recesses of the cave. When she finished the story with the burial, Moonflower spoke up.

"In the old days, Kachina, you and Grandmother Boo would have been called witches. It was said in those days that the only ones who lived in the ground were either animals or witches. With your Gift in the healing arts, and your connection with the spirit world – you would have been feared and shunned by our people. But there were none left to fear or shun you!"

She burst into laughter. "And the white men couldn't find you,' she added with difficulty.

Everyone in the room was laughing, including me. It was humor based on a small Indian victory in a period of their history dominated by defeat. It was pure Indian humor, so why was I laughing? I was white and had not remembered that when she said, "white men." I had reacted as an Indian!

Keechie then told them the story of the two hunters that had walked within yards of her while she was standing on the porch that her father had built.

"Dey nevva even look my way! Dey were close 'nuff I could hyer 'em breathin'! Hee, heeeee. Maybe I IS a witch! Hee, heeeee."

She could hardly catch her breath between peals of laughter.

"White man don' unnerstan' da spirits. Ol' Puma Man were watchin' out fer dis l'il Injun gurl dat day!"

Bearpaw wiped his eyes and said, "Kowakatcu, the Puma Man, has been directing all of our paths up to this moment. He directed Brian, our Yoholo here, to Kachina; then he led the two of them to this place. Then he led Long Walker to the square where these two were singing. He does not force anyone to do anything – he simply shows us new paths that are available. Whether we take these paths or not is up to us. The paths already taken seem to have been the right ones."

He paused and looked around the room. "Pumawoman, have you spoken to Kachina?"

"Yes I have, Uncle, and she accepts. And Yoholo?"

"Then I have an announcement to make. Yoholo, our new Storyteller and History Instructor, and Kachina, the Spirit Singer have both agreed to spend at least this summer with us. They will teach our children of our history and our culture. They bring new hope to our Nation." His voice filled with emotion as he spoke.

One old man broke the silence and shouted with upraised hands, "Kowakatcu! Kowakatcu!" as we would say, "Hurray! Hurray"!

Everyone answered with upraised hands, "Kowakatcu!"

The medicine bag beneath my shirt grew warm.

Chapter Nineteen
Osochi Corn

One of the most important ceremonies in the Creek culture was the Green Corn Festival, and it was to be held in two weeks. It marked the beginning of their New Year. Preparations were well under way, and the excitement was growing on the reservation. The "Stomp Dance Ground" was being cleaned and prepared for the eight-day festival. The beginning of the ceremony was the building of the "New Fire" which was started by a specially appointed fire maker who would use the old friction method with a bow driven drill and fireboard.

Keechie received the honor of being this year's Firestarter.

She was very pleased with the honor but admitted to me, "I sho wish dat I had Granny Boo's fire-maker. Dat would make her spirit ver' happy! Hit were her Granny's, an' I still got it! Only hit's in da cave back home," she said with disappointment.

"But Keechie, I've got to go back home for a week or so to spend some time with my parents. Do you want to stay here or go with me?

I will be back in time for the Green Corn ceremony, and I can bring whatever you want back with me."

"I sho din' know I wuz a'comin' hyer when I leff, an' I sho din' know I wuz gonna be gone da whole summer. Dey's a lot I needs t' do whut dey askin' me t' do hyer. I sho lak t' have my own stuff, so I 'spose I be goin' wit' you!"

What happened next would almost change her mind. Bearpaw told me about a government transport flight of the Bureau of Indian Affairs that would be going to Atlanta in a few days. It would be returning in a week with supplies and officials that would be present for the Green Corn Ceremony. There would be space for passengers, and we could fly home free! That would save at least two days of travel time by car and Keechie would finally have her chance to learn about airplanes!

Keechie was less than thrilled by that news, but reluctantly agreed.

"Puma Man done took me flyin', I speck I can do it one mo time… but I ain't sho I'se gonta like it!"

Long Walker drove us to the small airfield about twenty miles away. My parents agreed to meet us at Atlanta Hartsfield and take us home to Pine Mountain Valley. It was a converted transport plane with only eight passenger seats—the rest of the space being devoted to cargo. Keechie was very reluctant to climb aboard but finally, after conferring with the spirits, went up the steps, muttering under her breath the whole time.

The take-off was bumpy and loud. Keechie gripped the armrests with white knuckles, but still looked out the window as the ground dropped away beneath us. Reaching altitude, we turned due east as the sun sank below the horizon behind us.

It was nearly completely dark when we arrived over Atlanta. Dark enough for the city lights to be visible below. Keechie, who had never looked away from the window, said with astonishment, "Puma Man done showed me dis befo'! Hit's all da same!"

My parents were waiting at the terminal. I was suddenly overcome with emotion at the sight of them and I ran to greet them. Keechie was right there with me as we hugged and greeted each other.

On the way home we told them about the summer jobs that had been offered to us. Dad was very pleased and reluctantly admitted that he may have been wrong about me finding someone to "pay me for digging in the dirt."

"I'm proud of you, son, and thank you, Keechie. This wouldn't have been possible without you."

We spent that night and most of the following day with my family. Keechie was anxious to get to her cave, so in the early afternoon I drove her to the Rock. We climbed down and followed the familiar trail to her cave.

All was just as she had left it. She went into the storeroom and returned with Granny Boo's firedrill and bow. She took out a little bag of tinder and began the process of making a fire.

"I have a lighter, Keechie," I told her.

"Wants to see if I kin still do it the old way, Brine. 'Sides, a new far 'sposed t' be started dis way, an' I needs me a far. I don' nevva let it die out less'n I has to."

Soon she had a wisp of smoke rising from the hollow in the fireboard. She continued a bit, then quickly fed it with tinder while blowing gently on the spark. A flame burst forth, which she fed with larger twigs. She then transferred it to her hearth. Soon there was a nice fire blazing in the ancient fireplace, and she placed a pot of water on to boil.

"Been wantin' me some lemongrass and mint tea. I sho has missed dis place. Don' know how I'se goin' t'stay gone de whole summa, but hit sho wuz good t' be dere wit' m' fambly," she said.

"So I'se a witch, huh?" she added with humorous sarcasm.

"I knows some witch stuff, but I ain't never done dat but once. Hope I don' nevva have to do hit agin. Granny Boo say dat it usely come back t' da witch mo powful than hit leff."

I started to ask her about that 'one time' she had used the Gift for witching, but didn't. If she had wanted to tell me, she would have.

After a cup of tea, and talking about our recent adventure, I realized how late it was getting. The trip back up the mountain would be difficult after dark, so I told her I had to go.

"Will you come to my house with me, or would you rather stay here?"

I already knew the answer, but made the offer anyway.

"I needs t' stay hyer a few days, Brine. Got's t' 'cide whut I'se goin' t' take wit' me, n' whut I'se goin' t' hafta leave behind."

"I'll come back in a couple of days, Keechie. In five days, we will return to the reservation as Kachina the Firestarter and Yoholo the Storyteller. Are we ready for this?"

"Ready as we evva gone be, Yoholo. Puma Man done seed t' dat! Hee, hee!"

Two days later I returned. This time I followed the creek, the same as I had before I got a car. There was a nostalgic feeling about the old trail that led to the spring where I had met Keechie, six years past. It seemed longer than the promised two days since I had left her, and to be quite honest, I missed her.

When I came to the spring, I remembered the scare she had given me that first day. This time, however, there was no Keechie, and only the sounds of nature awaited me.

Neither was she outside the cave entrance as I approached the old porch. Calling out softly to her, I entered the cave. The hearth was warm, and a pot of water was simmering—but no Keechie was there to greet me. There was a pile of things near the entrance that hadn't been there two days ago, so she had collected the things she wanted to take back to the reservation, I presumed. But this was strange—she usually seemed to know when I was coming and would meet me.

The hairs on my neck raised in a sense of danger. I retrieved my bow and quiver of arrows from the storeroom, as the feeling of danger intensified. As soon as I left the cave, Puma Man appeared in my mind. He was looking down at a very familiar Rock, and immediately I knew where Keechie was —and that she was in danger.

Nearing the burial ground, I began "Injun Walkin", and made a wide circle instead of continuing straight ahead as I really wanted to. I thought I saw movement in the bushes between me and the Rock, but all was still. I moved in closer.

Then I heard them.

I had heard stories about the packs of wild dogs that roamed the area but I had never seen them. The deep-throated snarls that I heard told me that this was a large pack, and it was circling the Rock. Unslinging my bow and nocking an arrow, I began my approach from downwind.

One of the dogs briefly appeared between two trees but I had no time to react. Moving more cautiously now, I worked my way even closer, trying to watch behind me now as well.

The first thing I saw was Keechie standing on top of a huge boulder, with a large stick in her hands. She was holding it protectively in front of her.

Then I saw the dog. He was a huge, slavering, mangy looking beast, and was about to lunge at her. My arrow struck him through the neck just as he leaped at her, and he fell twitching at the base of the boulder.

Keechie yelled and pointed behind me. The second dog was almost on me, and there was no time to draw another arrow. The dog lunged at me from a full run and I fell to my back, drawing my knife as I went down. The dog passed over me and I laid its belly open as it went over me. It was still snarling and biting at me when I stabbed it through the heart. Looking over my shoulder, I saw Keechie swinging her stick at yet a third one.

This time I had time to nock another arrow and take aim. My arrow struck him between the shoulder blades just as he was about to leap at her. She jumped from the boulder and ran past me with her knife upraised.

The largest one yet had been stalking me from behind, and was now in full charge. It was at least twice her body weight, but she met it head-on as it leaped. The dog's weight and momentum struck her full on and carried her to the ground almost on top of me.

My heart stopped.

"Keechie!" I cried out in horror as I leaped to my feet and grabbed my knife again.

There was no movement from the huge beast, but it was lying on top of Keechie. Grabbing it around its neck, I rolled him off her. Her eyes were shining with blood lust as she pulled the knife I had given her from its throat.

She was immediately on her feet.

"Dey's mo," she said in warning, and turned to place her back to mine, prepared for the next onslaught. We must have killed the leader, for the remainder of the pack disappeared into the forest.

Several minutes later we felt safe enough to sit down and take stock of ourselves. We were covered with blood, but none of it was ours.

Adrenaline was still surging through my veins, and my hands were shaking as I wiped my knife off in the grass, and readied my bow again.

"I sho wuz glad to see dat arrow fly, Brine. Dey's hat me cornered up on dat rock most a' da mawnin'! I nevva even seed dem a'comin' 'til dey wuz on me. Must a' been least eight o' dem er mo, juss a'circlin' an' a'movin' in closer an' closer. You sho done save dis ol' woman's life, I thank."

Then she looked at the bow I was carrying.

"Whut made you brang dat bow wit' you?"

"Well, you weren't at the cave, and you always seem to know when I'm coming, and I was worried, and, well... I don't know! I just grabbed it as I left the cave to look for you. Then Puma Man came to my mind. He showed me where you were. Your Protector saved us both today!"

"I thank you right, Brine. Wait hyer. I gots juss da thang fer Puma."

She went to the base of the boulder, picked up her pack, and brought it back to where I was standing. Reaching inside, she brought out a pouch of tobacco and a pipe. She began a soft chant.

"You got fire?" she asked.

She lit the pipe and blew smoke to the four directions. Then she blew it to the sky, then to the earth, chanting the ancient verse as she did. She reached again into the pack and took out a second pouch. It was golden corn pollen, and she sprinkled it first into the air and then onto the two of us, while still chanting.

I offered my own thanks to the Puma Man silently, but very heartfelt.

She then began unceremoniously dragging the dogs' carcasses away from the burial ground.

"Don' even want dey blood in da same groun' as my people," she said with contempt.

"Dey's prolly juss hungry, but dey be evil. Bad spirits in 'em."

I retrieved my arrows from the two I had shot, but she stopped me from putting them back in the quiver with the others.

"Gots t' purify 'em firs'. Dey's got evil blood on 'em."

We walked back to her cave with a new appreciation for simply being alive. Everything seemed more vibrant and complete as we made our way through the natural beauty of the forest. All seemed in balance once more.

It was difficult leaving Keechie again, but she still wanted to remain at the cave. The next two days went by slowly. Finally, on Saturday afternoon I drove to the Rock to pick her up for our return trip to Oklahoma the next morning.

There, at the base of the Rock, was a pile of her stuff, all ready to go, and she was coming up the trail with another load.

"Dis de las' of hit. Leas' hit's evathang I kin thank of I'se gon' t' need."

We loaded up the car and drove back to my home where my

family was waiting. My mom and grandma had prepared a huge dinner for us as a "going away" party.

The next morning we were on our way to the airport. Because of our supplies, there was only room in the car for Dad and the two of us, so Mom told me good-bye at the house. We were on our way!

The return flight wasn't nearly as dramatic an adventure as the trip to here, but it was a day flight. Keechie enjoyed being able to see the landscape beneath us and was thrilled at being able to see clouds from the top.

Long Walker, Pumawoman, Bearpaw and Moonflower were at the small airfield to meet us with a car and a pickup, and made it obvious that they were genuinely happy to see us.

On the drive to their house, Keechie told Bearpaw about the incident with the dogs.

"Brine—Yoholo—he kilt two of 'em with arrows, and anotha one wit' 'is knife!"

"And Kechie killed the largest one of all with her knife. She saved my life!" I added.

"Seems the two of you saved each other's life to me. You make a good team!" Bearpaw smiled at us as we pulled into the driveway.

Long Walker took Keechie and I out to the Stomp Dance Grounds. There were separate areas set aside for games and campsites. Several tents were already set up and there was a bustle of activity. Newly built booths were ready for the food and refreshments, and one special one that held the new corn for the ceremony. This ritual would end the week long fast and then there would be roasted corn for all.

"This year's crop was disappointing," Long Walker said as he showed us the New Corn.

"First we had no rain for the newly planted corn, and then when the crop was maturing, we had too much."

Keechie looked over the baskets of the selected corn that he was showing us.

"Whut kinda corn is dis?" she asked as she picked up one of the ears.

"Hit ain't near as purdy as whut I grows. Mine come from far back as Granny Boo could 'member. I brung some o' it wit' me, fer seed an' safekeepin'."

Hearing those words, Long Walker looked at her in unconcealed astonishment.

In a hushed whisper he asked, "You have some of our People's original corn, Kachina?" then continued looking at her in eager anticipation.

"Sho I does. Whut you thank I been growin' all dese yars? I gots Bull Killer's daddy's corn. Hit's bigger dan dis! Got mo color too," she said, as she unceremoniously tossed the ear of corn back into the basket.

"Granny Boo say dat in de ol' days, dey din't 'low no udda corn t' be growed. She kep t' da ol' ways, so I does too!"

"Kachina, this may be the very reason Puma Man brought us together. If you have preserved the corn of our ancestors after all these years…"

His voice seemed to fail him as his mind apparently raced with the implications of Keechie's words…

He called Bearpaw as soon as we returned to his house. The Mico was there within minutes of the call. He seemed as excited as Long Walker and immediately asked Keechie if they could see the corn that she had brought.

Keechie went into her room and returned with one of her packs. Inside were over two dozen ears of dried corn.

"Hit's the onliest thang I wuz worried 'bout leavin'. Da critters love it as much as I does, an' I juss couldn't take da chance o' losin' it… Dis be Osochi corn," she said with pride as she handed each of them an ear.

"The old 'uns brung it wit' 'em from out west when dey firs' come 'cross da 'Hoochee, Granny Boo say."

Bearpaw, Long Walker and Moonflower looked at each other. They each held the ear of corn that Keechie handed them as if it were a priceless relic from the past.

To them it was.

" Kachina—Spirit Singer, this is the most wonderful thing that has happened since our tribe was driven from our ancestral lands. Many of our people brought corn with them on the Long Walk. Hunger forced them to either eat it or starve. Many of them starved anyway. All they had to begin anew was the corn that the government provided to them, but it was the white mans' corn."

"This...," Bearpaw said as he raised up the ear of corn he was holding, "...is the very heart and soul of our people—our culture. Our god has been returned to his people!"

There were tears in his eyes as he spoke again.

"We need to contact Michelle Fox, our horticulturist," he said as he tried to regain his composure.

Suddenly realizing that they had all assumed that Keechie had meant for them to have the corn, he asked sheepishly, "Kachina, may we take some of this corn?"

"Sho, you can have hit all. I gots mo. I brung it cuz o' da Green Corn thang, an' I din' wanna lose da seed, juss in case sompin' happen whilst I wuz gone. Hit were gonna be my offrin' anyhow. I got lots mo back at m' cave, whut don' gets et by de critters."

Michelle Fox, a local full-blooded Muskogee woman, finished college, received her degree in horticulture, and returned to her people. She arrived almost breathless after receiving Bearpaw's call.

She had not yet met Keechie, and went immediately to her and took her hands.

"I am honored to meet you, grandmother. If this is the original breed of maize that our ancestors brought to this land, then you have succeeded in doing something that many others have only dreamed of."

Keechie didn't seem to understand what all the fuss was about, but appeared to enjoy everyone's excitement.

"I jess kep' doin' whut my Granny Boo teached me."

"Kachina, there are many scientists trying to bring back the ancient maize that was developed in what we now call now Mexico. They even find it difficult to believe that our ancestors intentionally turned teosinte, a simple grass, into what we now call corn. May I see it?"

Keechie handed her an ear and seemed completely taken with the younger woman.

"Brine brung me some sto-bought cornmeal once. Hit were ground up all nice, but hit sho din' taste lak dis do! Dis be differnt somehow."

I remembered that evening so long ago that Keechie had brought in her last harvest of corn and we had roasted some to go along with those steaks. I had felt then that it was special, but never had a clue as to just HOW special it was.

Michelle looked at the ear closely. She gently pulled away part of the dried husk and studied the large yellow kernels.

"Thank Hesaketvmese, the Master of Breath, that you brought this here on a non-commercial flight. Otherwise, they probably would have prevented you from bringing it across state lines! No one looked into your bags, Kachina?"

"Nope. We juss got on dat airplane wit' our stuff an' 'way we went!"

Keechie seemed proud of herself for apparently breaking another of the "White Man's Laws."

"If this corn breeds true, and is not cross-pollinated with more modern varieties.... Kachina, Brian, how isolated are the fields where this was grown?" Michelle was now shaking out the remaining pollen from the ear onto a tissue.

Keechie looked puzzled at the question, so I replied for her.

"She has several small areas where she plants her corn. They are at the very foot of a mountain, about two miles from any other fields. The prevailing winds are west to east, blocked mostly by the mountain. If anything, her corn pollinates the other fields."

I knew what she was thinking – pollen from any other corn crops could have been carried in the wind and contaminated the ancient variety.

"I eats any that don' look lak it's 'sposed to. I keeps only da best fer plantin', lak Granny Boo teach me. I keeps dis too," she said as she took out a pouch from another bag.

"Dis be fer da spirits an' de Puma Man, whut I don' use when de tassels is ready. Hit come from only da best a' da best."

Michelle gingerly opened the pouch and looked inside.

She quietly announced with awe in her voice, "Our dear Kachina here has continued the work of our ancestors who gave us corn to begin with," and poured some of the contents out onto the tissue. It was the pure golden pollen from the Osochi corn.

There was a reverent silence in the room. Corn pollen was sacred among these people. They used it as an offering to the spirits, to their ancestors, and in any purification ritual. It was the Holy Water of the Catholics, and the Sacrament of Christianity.

"I have an experimental crop now that has not yet produced tassels. It was to be the last of this season's crop. With this...," she pointed at Keechie's pollen, "I can introduce this ancient strain into the new," she said excitedly.

"But with this," she said as she raised an ear of Keechie's corn to the room, "I can reproduce the original strain of maize that our ancestors created. Kachina, I grant you an honorary degree in Horticulture!"

Chapter Twenty
The Green Corn Festival

On the evening of the Green Corn Dance, the thoroughly cleaned central plaza was purified in a special ritual. As drummers began a slow rhythmic cadence, four young men entered the circle, called the *paskova*, and placed four large logs in the center for the building of the Sacred Fire.

Keechie, in her traditional outfit, slowly walked to the logs and with the help of Long Walker, carefully aligned them to the four directions. She took Granny Boo's fireboard, drill and bow from her pack. She raised the bow to the sky as the men and women, led by Bearpaw, began chanting along with the beat of the drums.

Kneeling beside the logs, she began the age-old process of creating the New Fire. After a few long moments, a wisp of smoke appeared from the fireboard and she paused to add tinder. Continuing to draw the bow back and forth, she appeared to be oblivious to the onlookers. She lay the bow down after a few more minutes and blew gently into the tinder. A flicker of flame appeared and she added yet more tinder. The crowd cheered as she placed the burning tender into the center of the logs.

Soon a large fire was burning and Bearpaw kindled a torch from it. Moving in a counter-clockwise circle around the perimeter of the circle, he led the chanting as it now changed to a heavier, more rhythmic pattern, defined by the stomping of the women's feet. The women had small pebble-filled turtle shells strapped to their ankles, which added a sizzling accompaniment to the rhythmic stomping. Then they began following him around the circle, alternating man, woman, man, woman, as they shuffle-stepped around the fire in their ancient, hypnotic ceremony.

Caught up in the ritual, I found myself next to Keechie, chanting along and feeling very fortunate to be a part of these wonderful people.

Several women brought out the freshly roasted new corn in steaming baskets.at the conclusion of the dance. Moonflower raised the first ear to the sky. She said some words in the old tongue, then tasted it. "It is good!" she cried, and the gathering again cheered because their fast was over. Everyone grabbed an ear of the new corn and the feasting began.

Bearpaw, Michelle Fox, Moonbeam and several other elders approached the podium. Bearpaw took the microphone and called for the attention of the crowd.

"My friends, my brothers and sisters of this great Muskogee Nation, I have a very important announcement to make. Our Firestarter this year, Kachina, who remained in our ancestral home in Georgia, has only this month found her family here. She is the great-granddaughter of Bull Killer. Her family, over the intervening years, has kept the original strain of maize that was lost to us on our journey here. She has honored the memory of her people that brought the first maize from Mexico so many centuries ago. She has kept the sacred rituals each year, even when she was the only one remaining of her family. Tonight, I am pleased to announce to you that she has brought that original maize with her and offers it as a gift to you, her people!"

When the cheering and applause had died down, Bearpaw took a small pouch from his pocket. He took a pinch of the golden pollen and placed it in his palm.

With a great shout of "Kowakatcu! The corn of the Osochi returns!" he blew upon his palm, sending the pollen out towards the people.

A sudden breeze sprang up, spiraling the pollen up into the air above the assembly, and glinting golden in the harsh light of the spotlights, it descended upon the people. They were silent, as the pollen descended upon them, then cheered again.

When he could again be heard, he said, "You all know Michelle Fox, our sister and horticulturist. She will fill you in on the plans for re-establishing our ancestral crop on this reservation."

Michelle took the stand and cleared her throat.

"Kachina has brought enough of the corn to start a small crop that will be used to produce enough seed to share with all. By next spring, we will produce enough for distribution throughout the reservation. She has also brought enough pollen to begin an experimental program that we will use to hybridize our present crops with the best characteristics of the old."

Taking a deep breath and looking out among her people, she continued.

"We must take great care to keep these strains separate and pure. Pollen from our present crops must not be allowed to pollinate the pure Osochi corn that Kachina has returned to us. When the seed is distributed in the spring, special instructions will be provided along with it."

She held an ear of Keechie's corn up and presented it to the crowd.

"Our God returns to his people!" she cried, and the assembled crowd again cheered.

People then began chanting, "Kachina, Kachina," with upraised hands, showing their appreciation for the woman who had saved the corn

Michelle looked around for Keechie. She was standing beside Moonflower near the stage, looking very small as Michelle motioned for her to join her on the stage.

Keechie walked up to the podium hesitantly, and with assistance from Bearpaw to adjust the height of the microphone said, "Hit's the only corn I evva hat. I din' know I wuz a'doin' anythang spechul, but I'se proud dat y'all 'preshate it. My Granny Boo say dat hit were better'n de white mans' corn, so I kep on a'growin' it."

She looked around nervously as the crowd cheered louder than before.

Bearpaw took the microphone from her, and holding one of her arms in the air announced, "Kachina will be staying with us this summer – hopefully longer. Welcome her, our grandmother, to your homes and our community as she teaches our young ones of the Old Ways."

Cries of "Kachina" echoed through the Stomp Grounds. My heart filled with pride for Keechie for her innocent adherence to tradition, for in doing so, she had preserved not only the corn, but also a huge part of her people's religion.

Keechie's gatherings became a legend on the reservation. Not only did the children attend her daily "classes", but their parents and older members of the Clans all found reasons to listen to her stories that she had learned from Granny Boo. The story of old Bull Killer was the most often requested, but any story she told was repeated until they became ingrained into the oral traditions of the many clans that made up the reservation.

Kachina, the Spirit Singer of the Puma Clan, became a legend among her people as well. Many years after her death the story of the woman who remained alone in their ancient homeland and had saved the corn was still being told with reverence and awe.

"Well, you see, hit seem dat evathang is juss part of evathang else. Rocks, trees, sky, dirt, animals, and peoples. The song jus' reminds all dose thangs dat dey is a part a' hit all, and dey's got dey

own job t'do. We be pre-shatin' it, an' we gots to let 'em know dat too. Evathang gonna come back aroun' 'ventual lak. Big ol' wheel be a'turnin'. Sometime you's at de top, but den you gots to take yo turn at de bottom, knowin' dat de Wheel gonna brang you right back up on top soon 'nuff."

Part II

Chapter One
Armageddon, American Style

I closed the old manuscript that I had been reading aloud to my daughter, Alexis.

"I finished writing that in my senior year of college," I told her.

"At first it was first just a kind of diary that I started to kill time whenever I got homesick. Then I made most of it into my college thesis. I made a good grade on it because of the things I learned from... Keechie."

There. I told her. I was sorry now that I hadn't told her about Keechie from the start, but the only other people in my family who knew about her, besides my wife, had died before she was born. First was my father, who died at a young fifty-two. Then my grandmother died at the age of seventy-two, and then my mother, who had passed away just two months before our daughter was born.

"I thought Brian sounded a lot like you, Daddy, but you never said you were the same Brian in the story! So it's real? The whole thing is about you and… wait! So Keechie is real too! She was my favorite person in your story! I feel like I know her."

"It's all true, baby—Keechie, her people—all of it. She would have loved you too. She was the most wonderful person you would ever want to meet. I think she knows about you too. She even said something once…"

I told her of the time when Keechie told me that I would have a daughter some day. Her voice echoed in my mind…

You's gonna have a girl child with de Gift, same as me an' Granny Boo. Puma done tole me dat too. She gonna make a differnce in dis worl'.

"Daddy, ever since you started reading me your book… well, I've been having these dreams… about Keechie and this man. He kinda looks like what I imagine the Puma Man in your story looks like. Is he real too?"

"He's real to me, sweetie. He is a kind of dream man, but he watches out for people who believe in him. Now you get to sleep. School day tomorrow."

I gave her a goodnight kiss and sat there with her until she drifted off to sleep. Memories flooded back from those times as I watched her lying there beside me.

Nearly fifty years had passed since I had first met Keechie. I was now living in a suburb of Atlanta, Georgia, seventy-five miles to the north of my old homeplace. I had that family that Keechie had foretold—a wife and daughter—the latter having been born when I was fifty years old and my wife, Mary, was thirty-four. We had a late start on children, but Alexis was worth the wait; but it was frightening raising a child in these troubled times.

The terrorist attack on the Twin Towers, the wars in Afghanistan and Iraq, kidnappings and videotaped beheadings, airport security, Homeland Security—all contributed to the uncertainty of our future. My daughter's future was much more uncertain than mine had ever been—and I had lived through the Cold War years under the threat of nuclear war with the USSR

George W. Bush was elected for his second term. Terrorism had become a way of waging war that far surpassed the fear factor of anything I had ever lived through. No one was safe. Any public gathering became a potential target. There was no uniformed enemy to wage war upon. Women and children were not exempt as targets—in fact, they were preferable because their killing raised the fear factor—and this was the sole intent of the enemy.

It was only two weeks after I had read my manuscript to Alexis that it began...

First, there were a few cases of an unknown disease, similar to Ebola, detected in several major cities across America. The authorities could only trace them to "persons unknown" traveling by major airlines. The passenger lists were large and the potentially exposed victims were too numerous to count.

Then came the suicide bombers to cities great and small all across the land. Always striking at large crowds, they only used very small explosive charges strapped to their bodies. The explosions themselves didn't cause much physical damage—usually just the bomber was killed outright, but everyone else in the crowd was sprayed with blood, body fluids and parts.

The spread of the mystery disease intensified. The Centers for Disease Control in Atlanta was now as secure and closely guarded as the White House. A State of National Emergency was declared and Martial Law enacted. Homeland Security, made up of people only minimally trained in airport security went into action. They, guided mostly by panic, acted without adequate instruction or direction. Fortunately, a vast majority of these ill-trained "professionals" deserted the ranks in fear for their own lives.

Then, as the public panic reached its maximum, the power grids were sabotaged across the land. Communication systems failed. Radio and television, so secure with their "Emergency Broadcasting System" went off the air. Cities and rural areas alike were in the dark. Water purification plants shut down. No stores were open. No airlines were flying. No trucks were making deliveries. The remaining fuel could not be pumped from the storage tanks.

There was no public transportation, and the sick and dying went uncared for. Hospitals remained open until the fuel for their emergency generators ran out; then the medical staff, fearing for their own lives and those of their families, failed to report for duty. The patients who were able to leave did so. Many of them, too sick to leave, died in the dark, deserted by those entrusted with their care.

Mass panic ensued, and mobs ran through the streets, stealing anything they could find. Money was useless, while food, guns, ammunition, drugs and antibiotics became the new currency.

The military began closing down all major routes into and out of the cities. They quarantined entire neighborhoods where the sickness seemed worst. Local governments enacted strict curfews, but due to the lack of personnel, they were not adequately enforced.

I had already prepared my emergency supplies. Ever since the Y2K scare, I had been stocking my "Grab Bags", and they had been maintained and added to ever since. Without the knowledge of my family or any other living soul, I had safely deposited the larger portions of these supplies in a certain cave in a place that was far, far away from any city.

We closed down our home, gathered our remaining necessities and valuables, and loaded up my pickup.

"Where are we going, Daddy?" my precious eleven-year-old Alexis wanted to know, looking at me with that same intensity and trust she had shown just after the 9-11 attacks.

Just before all flights were suspended, she had watched an airplane fly over and, in a fearful voice, asked me if it was "one of them."

"To Keechie's cave, darling. Remember my story? The government forced the rest of her tribe to go to the reservation, while. Keechie and her family remained safely hidden there all those years. No one ever knew she was there until I discovered her at the spring."

I looked across the cab of my truck at my wife of 27 years and gave her a smile.

"I love you two more than my own life," I told them as we pulled out of the driveway of the home we had shared for all these years.

"We'll be okay. I promise you both."

I pulled away from the curb praying to any God who was listening that I could keep that promise.

I took all the back roads south to my old homeplace and the mountain that I so loved. I had planned the time of our leaving so that we could arrive a couple hours before sunset. We were far enough from Atlanta that the greater part of the mob activity had not begun in full force.

We only saw a few small groups of people along the roads, who yelled at us to stop, but I sped past them. There was nothing I could do to help them, and besides, the safety of my family came first.

We were heading for Pine Mountain... and to Keechie's cave.

Chapter Two
Our New Home

The road across the top of the mountain was deserted as we approached the old, overgrown trail that led to the Rock. I drove past it the first time just to make sure no one saw us turn in. The brush was almost as high as the hood of my truck, and only those who knew that the road was there would attempt it.

At its end, I drove a little further and parked between two bushy scrub oaks. After we had removed our supplies, I planned to cover the truck with branches and make it as inconspicuous as possible.

We stood at the top of the Rock as the sun was sinking low in the west, directly behind us. We would be still in sunlight standing here, while the valley below would be in darkness, shadowed by the mountain

"This valley may be our home for a while, girls. I hope you like it as much as I do," I told them as I watched their expressions as they took in the view.

Please, God, let this be the right decision I have made, was my fervent prayer.

I began unloading the truck and carrying the supplies to the head of the trail down the mountainside. I carried only those things that we would need first to the base of the Rock. The rest we carefully concealed beneath limbs and leaves for later retrieval. I wanted to get my family settled into the cave as soon as possible, with as many of the necessities as we could transport, before darkness fell.

Over the years since Keechie's death, I had stocked the cave well with emergency rations, extra lamps, kerosene and medical supplies. My friends had jokingly called me a "closet survivalist" just from my preparations I had made at home. Little did they know just how close to the truth they had been. The cave would have confirmed their jokes. It had been two years since my last visit and I hoped that it was still secure—which reminded me to take precautions as we approached the entrance.

"Y'all wait right here and be very quiet for a minute. I want to check things out first."

I circled the entrance cautiously, drawing my wife's Colt .380 in the process. I didn't want any surprises, like someone else had found the cave and taken up residence.

After Keechie died, I had removed the old porch and roof from the opening and strategically planted two mountain laurels in front of the opening. I never fully understood why no one had ever found it before, but I knew that Puma Man had something to do with it.

No sign of occupation was evident, but I still used caution as I entered the dark cave. I felt for the lantern I had left near the entrance and lit it. All seemed to be just as I had left it.

"Thank you, Keechie and all your ancestors. Puma Man, protect my family as you protected them," I said aloud to the empty room.

Not as empty as it appeared, for the memories and spirits of Keechie and her clan seemed to be welcoming me. I felt like I had come home.

"Everything's okay," I called from the entrance. "You can come on down now."

They entered the cave slowly, unsure of what they were about to see. I lit a second lamp and showed them around the main room.

"This is really neat, Dad. I was expecting a hole in the ground!" Alexis said as she approached the fireplace.

"Is this where you and Keechie cooked the rabbit stew?"

"Yep, and the steaks, and the venison, and all that stuff I read to you. This was Keechie's home. She had everything she needed here."

We spent the next hour or so cleaning out the cobwebs and blown-in litter, and I made a fire in the hearth.

"Tomorrow I will show you where Keechie and all her ancestors are buried. We walked past them just now, but I was in a hurry to get us here safely first."

I checked the storeroom and saw that all the supplies that I had stored were still safe, waiting for us. One entire wall was filled with canned goods. The dried beans, flour, cornmeal and other moisture sensitive things were sealed in airtight containers. I had figured that if I could supplement the food supplies I had here with fresh game, we had enough to last us at least two years.

By then, if the need was still present, we could live as Keechie had for her entire life. I hoped that she had taught me well.

As we prepared our meal in the ancient hearth, Alexis asked me to tell her more about Keechie.

"I loved her as a character in your book, Dad. Knowing she was real makes me love her even more. It feels like she's here now, watching over us."

I had felt the same sensation ever since we arrived at the Rock.

I could almost hear her saying, *"Hee, hee, Brine, I juss knowed you wuz a'comin' back!"*

Puma Man and Granny Boo were here too. I could feel their presence, like a protective shield around us, and it was a comforting feeling.

Mary seemed as anxious as my daughter to hear the stories again. She had known about Keechie from the beginning of our marriage, but had considered her just a part of my childhood. Now she had entered our lives as the most important person I had ever known. Our chances of survival had been increased a hundred fold by her cave, her survival skills that she had passed on to me, and now it seemed, by her spirit that was watching over us.

"Well, Keechie would be saying right now, 'Dis is purdy good stew, but hit sho need mo salt!'" I joked, as I tried to think of a good, comforting story to tell my family. This was the most trying time of our lives, and we all needed some positive, inspirational thoughts as we spent our first of many, many nights in Keechie's cave.

"Keechie once told me that the spirits of her ancestors and the Puma Man guarded her and this cave. I had been worried about the porch and roof that her father had built over the entrance, that it was too obvious for a hunter or hiker to not see. Apparently, Puma Man and her ancestor's spirits blinded their eyes.

She said that once when she was a little girl, a couple of hunters had walked within a few yards of her while she was standing, frozen with fear, on the porch. They never even looked in her direction! That feeling that we have right now may be those same spirits, still watching over us. Now let's all get some sleep. We've got a lot of things to do tomorrow."

I banked the coals in the hearth just as Keechie had done and spread out our sleeping mats. We had everything we needed to survive that I could think of. More importantly,. we had each other. My family was safe and snuggled in beside me.

The world had changed around us and would probably never be the same again. Keechie's and her people's way of life had once again made the "Big Wheel" cycle that she had explained to me all those many years ago, and was now ours to learn.

"Thank you, Keechie," I said as I drifted off to sleep.

Thunder woke me around midnight. I eased out from under the blankets and went to the door. Lightning flashed and lit the landscape as I stepped outside. It had not yet begun raining, but you could smell it in the night air.

I sat on a large boulder, watched the storm brewing and thought about Keechie and her clan. The life my family and I were about to begin was their every day existence. They would have been far better equipped to survive today than most of the world's population, but they had been considered heathens and savages for living the way they did. I just hoped that I could remember all the things she had taught me.

Puma Man's voice spoke through the thunder.

"Things learned are never forgotten; when you need it, first you must remember the one who taught you."

At that instant, Keechie appeared to me in my mind. She was smiling and clasping the medicine bag around her neck. The one that was just like the one I still wore. I reached for it, held it tightly, and knew that we would survive this, and the world would heal.

The rain came suddenly and heavily. I went back inside and slipped under the blankets. I slept soundly until dawn came with a freshness that is only felt after a cleansing rain. I went to the fireplace and stirred the coals to build the fire up.

The coffee was ready just as my wife and daughter awoke. We prepared a good breakfast of bacon, grits and powdered eggs. Alexis was eating silently, so I asked her if she was okay.

"I'm fine, Dad, and dese is purdy good grits, but dey sho need mo salt! Hee, hee," she said with a big grin.

Later I took them both into the storeroom and showed them the relics of Keechie's people. They were as stunned as I had been when I first saw them. I had cleared two walls of the room for supplies and the boxes were piled to the ceiling. There were even more supplies in deeper recesses of the cave that I would show to them later. Especially important for them now was the pool of water behind this room. It was our primary source of fresh water and our key to survival.

"Will you two be okay alone here for a while, or do you want to go with me to get the rest of our stuff that we brought?"

I wasn't comfortable leaving them alone, and was relieved when they both volunteered to go with me. They also needed to be shown how to practice caution when entering and exiting the cave. No one must ever see us and discover this place

On the way up the trail, we made a game out of the art of "Injun Walkin", and I soon had them doing it fairly well.

We had covered the supplies with a tarp, so they were in good condition in spite last night's rain. It would take several trips, but we had all day to transfer them to the cave.

Just as we got to the base of the Rock, and I was about to show them the "Burrin' Ground", the sound of an engine cranking above us froze us in our tracks.

I motioned to them to get behind the rocks and to keep very quiet. Quickly climbing to the top of the Rock, I just had time to hear a vehicle leaving. It was at the main road, so whoever it was had not pulled down into the access trail where my truck was parked. It was well-hidden and hopefully, whoever it was had not seen it. Maybe they had not even been down the trail, but I feared it was hunters.

While carrying our first load back to the cave, my fear was confirmed. Through the middle of one of the clearings was a set of fresh boot prints heading up to the Rock. Alongside the bootprints were fresh deer tracks.

Fortunately, as part of my "Injun Walkin" lessons, we had avoided leaving any obvious footprints in these open areas. We had skirted the clearing each time we passed it, so our presence was not detected by the hunter. At least that is what I hoped. We had heard no gunshots since we had arrived, so he had left empty-handed.

His bootprints, after leaving the clearing, veered away from the cave and headed northward. Then I found two sets of the same prints, one set in each direction. He had come and gone by the same path. We had been very fortunate in missing him by only minutes, but he had surely seen the deer tracks. I had to assume that he would be returning to hunt the area.

On the final trip up to the Rock, I showed them the burial ground.

"Keechie is right here, between Granny Boo and her mother," I said, pointing at the spaces between the boulders.

"And right up there is old Bull Killer."

Alexis walked over to Keechie's spot and gently touched the stones. She was silent… just standing there for a moment; then she turned to us.

"Keechie is glad we are here. I can just feel it."

With this trip, we finished transferring the supplies. After we had everything organized and put away, we sat and discussed our new circumstances, and how we were going to deal with everyday life. My daughter's education had abruptly ended. We all laughed when Mary made a wry comment suggesting that we could begin "Cave Schooling."

We had considered home schooling many times in the past, and now it was the only choice we had. Several of the boxes I had previously stashed away in the cave contained most of my old textbooks, encyclopedias, and many of the great classics of literature. She would not be without an education.

We still had some communication with the "outside world". I had a battery-powered shortwave receiver and transmitter and a portable solar panel recharging system. Ham operators always found a way to talk. In times of national or local emergencies, they had proven themselves invaluable.

Rarely transmitting, I listened in frequently. This was our only contact with the situation across America, and tonight I was planning to catch up on the news.

We had brought our laptop computer with us, but it was useless for communication, because the Internet was down. Besides, we had no telephone lines to connect to anyway; but it was well stocked with saved files and CD's of all types, and could be useful in home schooling. It is also the word processor that I am using to record these events! It was another burden on the solar panels, but well worth it.

The visibility of the solar panels was a serious concern. There was no way to conceal them effectively, so we could not leave them in place continuously. They consisted of two four-by-six foot panels when fully opened. If they were seen, they could lead anyone directly to our cave like a neon sign proclaiming, "We Are Here."

It was a necessary risk we would have to take.

Chapter Three
Making Bones

On our second week at the cave, the inevitable happened. It had snowed lightly during the night and I had gone out early to try to get a deer. Having had no luck by mid-morning, I headed back to the cave, skirting the entrance in a wide circle to avoid leaving tracks in the snow.

I first heard his voice coming from the direction of the cave. He sounded angry but I couldn't make out his words. As I moved in closer, making my way to a point slightly above the entrance I could see him about twenty yards in front of me. He was no one I remembered from the area, but I had been away for a while... but now he had my wife and daughter tied up, sitting against a boulder, and was pointing his deer rifle at them.

"Where's yo daddy? Where you staying? How'd you git hyer?"

He slung his rifle over his shoulder and grabbed my daughter.

Pressing his hunting knife to Alex's throat, he demanded from my wife, "Now you'll tell me, or the girl's dead!"

The last thing he ever heard was the whirring of a crossbow bolt. The 18-inch aluminum bolt struck him in the center of his forehead and he went down instantly. I felt numb as I untied them and checked to see if they were all right. I had never taken a human life before, and my mind was racing. My first concern was my family. They were both silent and seemed more angry than anything. After a long family hug, I sent Alexis inside for a blanket to cover the man's body.

Mary, in a rush of words, said, "We had just gone out for some firewood and to see the snow. He just walked up. At first he seemed pleasant enough, but when we wouldn't answer his questions, he...."

She began crying—long sobs that racked her body. "I wasn't so afraid for me, but he was rough with Alexis. I think he would have..."

"I know, darling, I know. I'm just glad I came back when I did. I have never killed a man before, but he's the one that made that choice. I just hope he was alone. Maybe y'all should go back inside while I figure out what to do now. I know I've got to find his car or truck and move it or hide it or something. He's probably the same one who made those tracks we saw before, so I know where he most likely parked. Go inside now and get warm. I'll be in shortly."

As soon as they left, I checked over the body. The crossbow bolt had gone completely through his skull and the steel hunting point was protruding about two inches from the back of his head. I unscrewed the point and withdrew the bolt.

He had no identification on him and there was nothing in his pockets but an almost empty flask of whiskey, a box of 30-30 ammo, his keys and a compass. In his jacket pocket, I found a topographical map of the area. That was somewhat reassuring, because I figured that anyone who was from this area would not need a map.

I removed his boots and placed them aside, then covered him with the blanket, then with snow, and went back inside to my family.

"I've got to find and move his vehicle," I told them.

"I hate to leave y'all now, but this has to be done quickly, before it is spotted by anyone that may be looking for him. It would lead them right here. I'll have to hike back, so I may be a while."

About to remind Mary to keep her Colt automatic ready, I saw that would be unnecessary. She had it in her hand and was racking a round into the chamber.

As she placed the safety on and let the hammer down, she said, "Don't worry about us. Just be sure to let us know when you get back. "That…" she said, meaning the surprise attack from the hunter, "…will never happen again."

There were several places I knew of that were likely hunting areas and that was my plan. Let anyone who may be looking for him think he was hunting in a completely different area. There was one place in particular I was thinking of. It was near my old homeplace, and downstream from the spring where I had met Keechie. It was also on the opposite side of the road, and would lead any searchers in the opposite direction. Another advantage was that it wasn't so far that I couldn't get back to my family before dark.

There it was, just as I had thought—an old pickup parked just off the main road at the top of the Rock. The license plate was from Habersham County in north Georgia. Relieved, I took out his keys and got behind the wheel. The gas gauge indicated just over a half-tank. That was more than necessary for what I had planned, and we may need the gas. I found an empty five-gallon container in the back of the truck, and, not surprisingly, a section of hosepipe. I siphoned the container full, and stashed it on the trail near my truck.

I started the engine and pulled out onto the deserted highway. As I drove, I looked around inside the cab for anything that might identify him. It was unusually devoid of anything like that. There were no service tickets, letters, bills, or junk mail, which normally accumulated in everyone's vehicle.

The road was devoid of any other vehicles all the way to the turn down into the valley, but as I started down the mountain, I spotted another pickup truck heading up the mountain in a curve below.

An old sawmill road was coming up on my right, allowing me just enough time to turn in and go just far enough to be unseen from the main road. I killed the engine just as the truck went past and on up the mountain.

It was only a short distance now to the base of the mountain and the bridge that crossed the creek below my old home.

There was a cattle gate across the farm road that went alongside the creek. Quickly jumping out and opening the gate, I pulled the truck through, then closed the gate behind me.

An old hedgerow, a little further downstream, made the perfect place to park the truck. It would be unseen from the road, and since there were no cattle in the pasture, there was no reason for the owner to discover it.

Now I had time to check out the interior of the truck more thoroughly. The glove compartment was empty except for an old greasy owner's manual. Beneath the seat on the driver's side, I found an unopened fifth of Kentucky bourbon and his wallet, which contained twenty-three dollars in bills, but again there was nothing in the way of identification. It was apparent that this guy was intentionally travelling incognito.

I placed the wallet back under the seat just as I had found it. There were several more boxes of 30-30 ammunition behind the seat, along with two boxes of .380 hollowpoints – but where was the weapon?

I found it under the seat on the passenger side. It was identical to the one Mary was holding now. I had bought it as a birthday gift for her several years before. It was a Colt .380 automatic. This one would make a nice addition to my already large arsenal, and the extra ammunition made it all the nicer.

Giving the interior one more final sweep, I removed the keys from the ignition and rolled up the windows. I could now remove the gloves that I had worn since this whole thing started this morning. I took his boots from the bed of the truck and put them on —with an intense feeling of revulsion.

I made a few trips around the truck, then walked directly toward the creek bed, leaving as many tracks as possible. Following the creek for a couple hundred yards, I crossed to the other side. Walking directly away from the creek, I headed uphill to a grove of hickory trees, where I had spent many happy afternoons squirrel hunting when I was younger.

I sat and rested a bit while I removed his boots, replacing them with my own soft moccasins. "Injun Walkin" directly towards the creek, away from the huge old trees, I concentrated on leaving no tracks. I tried to think of anything I had forgotten. Instead of heading directly upstream to the truck, I made a wide circle and approached it from a different direction.

After I picked up the fifth of whiskey, which we would add to our medical supplies, the Colt automatic and the boxes of ammunition, I began the hike back to Kechie's cave, and to my family. I crossed the road by going underneath the bridge, and followed the creek upstream, just as I had done so many times in my youth. It was a very familiar path – the one that had had led me to Keechie so many years before. I paused at the spring, smiling as I recalled those very first words I heard from her.

Dat wada give you de shits for sho. You gots ta bile it furs'.

When I approached the cave entrance, I called out softly to my family, not wanting to frighten them. Besides, I did not want to be shot with that .380! Mary was quite good with it, and after the morning's events, she would not hesitate to use it.

They both met me at the entrance with warm, very welcome hugs. Our first trial by fire had been overcome.

On my way in, I had reluctantly glanced over to where the body lay, and had seen that the afternoon sun had melted the snow away from the blanket. My day was not yet over.

I made a travois out of the blanket, and dragged the body to the low-lying swampy area that Keechie had shown me. It was where her family buried their dead until there were only bones left.

Mary and Alex followed behind with pine branches, sweeping the trail I was leaving.

"Y'all go on back to the cave and start getting supper ready. This won't take long, and I'm getting hungry as a bear," I told them, giving my wife a "please humor me" look.

Digging a narrow trench into the wet ground, I dug as deeply as possible, until water began filling the hole. I removed all his clothes and placed him into the trench, covering him with flat slabs of sandstone. Then I replaced the earth on top; carefully concealing the area with leaves and twigs.

I Gathered his clothes into a bundle and carried them back to the cave, where they would be burned along with his boots.

They had a feast waiting on me. From what they had been through today, it seemed that staying busy was helping them cope, and they had been very busy.

We had a stock of dried, salted beef, and they had made a huge pot of stew, complete with beans, potatoes, carrots and onions. It was delicious! We sat and discussed the day's events for nearly an hour. It was best to get all the feelings and emotions out in the open, not only for their benefit, but for mine.

Knowing what I had done had been forced upon me did not change the fact that today I had taken another human life. What was bothering me the most was the fact that I felt no remorse for my actions. It seemed they were taking this with much more bravado than I was, and Alex went to sleep sitting in my lap.

I gently placed her under her blankets and looked into her peaceful sleeping face. I recalled the mind-numbing fear I had felt this morning when she had a knife at her throat. All of the guilt that I thought I should be feeling disappeared in a heartbeat.

My family was safe.

Mary and I went outside where I showed her the articles that I had removed from the truck.

"It's just like mine!" she said as she took the Colt from my hands.

"This is great! Now we both have one! And, just in case you're wondering, I put his deer rifle and ammo in the storeroom."

We sat there in the shadow of the mountain, holding each other for a long time, letting the horror of the day go. It now belonged to the past; while our future, as uncertain as it was, had been given another chance.

Chapter Four
Our First Year

After the assault on my family, it was difficult for me to leave them, even for short periods of time. However, necessity has a way of forcing things upon you. We still needed fresh meat, and I had yet to provide it. A week had passed and we had seen no indications that anyone was looking for the hunter, or even that anyone else was in the area.

One morning I woke early and gathered the things I would need to set rabbit traps. Mary was watching me from her blankets as I was getting my coat on, and I assured her I would be gone no more than an hour.

"Go back to sleep, honey. I'm just going to set a few traps. I'll be back before you get the coffee ready."

Keechie had shown me where to set the traps, and where the major game trails were. Many of them were near the spring, and that was where I was heading.

I no longer went anywhere without my crossbow, and today was no exception. I had it slung over my shoulder as I approached the spring. There were fresh signs of deer on the trail, so I prepared a bolt and cocked the bow. The little spring had frozen over, but I saw no signs of activity as I set the first trap.

A few yards further to the north, a small hickory tree looked promising for a snare. As I bent it down to make the second trap, I heard the "whuffing" sound of a deer from behind me. I knew that if I made any noise or motion it would be gone before I could even turn to see it, so I froze in my tracks. A moment later I heard the crunch of frozen snow from the direction of the spring.

The crossbow was cocked and ready, so I slowly began raising it as I turned. It was a young buck, with only two antler points showing. He was pawing at the frozen surface of the spring. He never saw me as I raised the crossbow to my shoulder and released the bolt. It struck him just at the "vee" of his collarbone. He made one jump away from the spring and fell, his legs twitching in a death throe.

Approaching him cautiously, I nudged him with my boot. There was no reaction so I made the necessary cut to his jugular vein and drug him to a position where his head was lower than his heart.

I had no rope to suspend him with, so I had to make another trip back to the cave. While I was gathering the rope, I made too much noise and woke Mary and Alex.

"Sorry I woke you, but get dressed and build up the fire. We have fresh meat!"

"Meat? You got fresh meat?" my daughter asked, rubbing the sleep from her eyes.

"Venison, baby. But I've got to hurry. Don't want to lose it to predators. Get dressed and we'll cut it up as soon as I can get it back. Start the coffee!"

Memories of Keechie flooded my brain as I raised the deer up into the tree and began the process of field dressing. Those thoughts reminded me to thank the deer for his sacrifice, and for the meat that would sustain my family.

God, I missed that woman, but she had never really left me. We were living in her world now. We were using the survival skills that she had taught me, and we seemed protected by her spirit and that of the Puma Man. These were all her gifts to my family and me, and they made Keechie seem almost as alive now as she had ever been.

As I retrieved my bolt from the deer, I wondered if Keechie would have accepted this as a kill by "bow an' arrow." That had been one of her favorite stories to tell when she was bragging about me on the reservation.

When I removed the liver, I cut a small piece and ate it, just as she would have done.

After removing the hide and internal organs, the carcass probably didn't weigh more than seventy pounds, so I carried it whole back to the cave. They were waiting outside for me with a cup of coffee.

Alex wanted to help with the butchering, so we began cutting the meat into smaller, more manageable pieces. We left the front and hindquarters whole, to be used as roasts; but the rest we cut into thin strips for smoking and making into jerky. No outside fire would be necessary. It could all be done over the hearth inside.

Then I remembered the old food grinder my mom had given Keechie. She had treated it almost as an object of worship since discovering it within the bags my mom had prepared for her. She and I mounted it to a board for a base; and it still sat beside the fireplace, covered by an old cloth apron.

We could make sausage instead of jerky… if only I had something to use as casings… and I did! One more trip to the spring was necessary anyway to bury the entrails, so I left again for the spring, this time carrying only a small shovel and of course, the crossbow.

I removed the small intestines from the pile of offal and buried the rest. A careful washing with water and they would make ideal casing for stuffing the sausage.

Mary prepared the seasoning for the sausage, then Alex and I ground the meat once, then added the seasoning. We placed the casing attachment onto the grinder, slipped the casings over the tube, and made the final grinding. Thank goodness my mom had included that special attachment for the grinder! Alex turned the handle, while I fed the meat into the grinder and controlled the amount that went into the casings.

I had not learned this skill from Keechie. My dad gets the credit for this one. He had taught it to me early on in my years at the old "Sto", except there, the grinder was electric and the casings were pork. Called "Chitlins" if cooked and eaten, and "casings" if they were to be used for making sausage, they were still the small intestines of an animal.

"Ain't nothing on a pig wasted," my dad had said to me at least a thousand times, "… except the oink!"

We looped the links of sausage over a green hickory limb that we suspended over the fireplace, so that the smoke and heat would cure them slowly. Mary took some of the links and cooked them as soon as we were finished. It was delicious with grits, and even the powdered eggs tasted wonderful. We felt a sense of pride and accomplishment just knowing that nature will provide for those willing to learn.

Our daily lives took on a routine not much different from what we had left behind, if you really thought about it. The lack of television, the invasive telephone and my addiction to the Internet, we replaced with family discussions, reading good books and practicing handicrafts.

Every evening we listened to the shortwave radio for an hour or so for news of the world situation. The terrorist attacks were continuing, but on a smaller scale. Nowhere on the earth was unaffected, but America, the leader in technology and the "better life", was the hardest hit.

We had been the least prepared to live without all the modern conveniences. Consequently, we suffered the most. Those who reacted by joining the mobs in the streets placed themselves in even greater danger. People were killed for their food, then the thieves were killed for what they had stolen. As terrible as the news was, it made us that much more fortunate to be where we were, away from all the madness.

By early spring I had chosen the seed that we would be planting from my stored supplies. I had already decided on the locations where the corn, beans and squash would be planted. These three crops were the sustenance of Keechie's people for centuries, so we couldn't go wrong there. Anything else we grew would be like icing on the cake. As Keechie had taught me, I didn't plan any large plantings in any one given place, but spread them out over several locations in a random, more natural pattern. A laid-out cornfield would be a dead giveaway that there were people living in the area, and our safety depended on our remaining unseen and unknown.

The Osochi corn that Keechie had preserved was to be our gift back to the original inhabitants of this area. I had safely stored it in airtight containers in the coolest recesses of the cave. It was important to me on a spiritual level to retain this corn and no other. I had no way of knowing how long it would remain viable, but I had taken every precaution to preserve it. I took a few kernels and placed them in water two weeks before planting time, to see if they would still germinate. Within days I knew that my efforts were not in vain. Nearly one hundred percent had germinated. Also to my advantage, I had found a large soft leather bag of Keechie's pollen. With that, I could be certain that the original strain would remain pure.

We made our first plantings on a beautiful, crisp spring morning. I remembered where Keechie planted her corn, so it was easy to decide where ours would be located. We planted it first, and after the young shoots reached about six inches in height, we would plant running pole beans beside each cornstalk, so they could climb them as they grew.

Later in the season, we would plant the squash in various places near the cave, and at the perimeters of open areas. Mary was thrilled at the herb seed I had stored, and she prepared a small kitchen garden near the cave.

Keechie would have been proud of us. We were continuing the way of life she had lived, and it was her knowledge that made it possible.

One summer evening, after we finished our evening meal of freshly caught rabbits and settled in for the night, Alex asked to hear the story of Keechie's death.

"That part wasn't in your book, Daddy. It ended with the Green Corn Festival. Why did you stop writing there?"

"I tried many times to write that part, baby. Somehow it just never came out right. It's hard to put those kind of feelings into words, so I just kept them in my heart."

I thought back over those last few years with Keechie. This final unwritten chapter of my life with the old Spirit Singer should not be left untold, so as we sat there in front of Keechie's hearth, I told them the story of Keechie's last few years...

Keechie and I stayed that whole summer after the Green Corn Festival. She was always torn between remaining on the reservation with her people, or staying here where her ancestors were buried. This was the only home she had ever known, and she loved it intensely.

We made many trips back and forth between here and the reservation, usually riding the government planes that made the trip frequently. On one of our trips back here, Long Walker came with us, fulfilling his childhood dream of coming here, to where his ancestors had been driven from. Remember that's where he got his name? He stayed here with Keechie in this cave for several days. He got to see and hold Bull Killer's spear just as I had, and honor his ancestors at the burial ground.

He died on the reservation that following summer just after the Green Corn Festival. He was about the same age as Keechie, and we were both there for his burial.

Every winter Keechie and I came back here for two weeks at Christmas, then we returned to the reservation. Keechie assisted Pumawoman with her duties as Healer and continued telling the stories of her people who had remained here. I taught at the local school and continued my research into their culture, origins, and migration routes into this New World.

We continued this for several years, going back and forth, the trips here becoming shorter and shorter, but Keechie still wanted to live here. She told me once that she wished that she could bring the whole reservation back here with her!

She was now around seventy-five years old and beginning to show signs of old age. We had come home for the Christmas holidays in 1976, two years after my father died. I had left her here at the cave for two nights while I visited my family. When I returned to check on her, and to begin collecting her things for our return to the reservation, she didn't meet me outside as she usually did.

I found her wrapped in her blankets in front of this hearth, trying to make a pot of tea. She could barely sit up, so I made the tea for her and helped her drink it.

Then she asked me to bring her Granny Boo's Power Bundle from the storeroom. I brought it to her and she held it tightly as she lay back down. I sat up all that night, watching her as she drifted in and out of sleep.

She seemed to be dreaming, murmuring in her sleep as if she was carrying on a conversation with someone that I couldn't hear or see, and when she did awake, her mind seemed to be still locked in her dream world.

Suddenly, just before sunrise, she sat bolt upright, still clutching Granny Boo's Power Bundle, pointed towards the ceiling and said excitedly, "Hit's Puma an' Granny Boo! Dey wants me to go wit' 'em!"

She lay back down, smiling peacefully, and by the time I could get to her, she was gone. Just like that. I reckon she left with Puma Man and Granny Boo. I closed her eyes and held her until the sun rose and I could deal with my grief enough to think of what I must now do.

She had already told me where she wanted to be buried.

"You' doesn't haf' t' wait t' get m' bones, Brine, lak in da ol' days. Just put me up dere lak we did my Pap an' my brother."

I sewed her body up in a beautiful deerhide robe that she had made. Then I went to the burial ground and prepared that space I showed you. She had picked that spot herself. It was where two large boulders stood about two feet apart.

After I removed the loose rubble and small stones between them, it created an opening several yards deep, until it looked like a small cave. I made a travois out of blankets and placed Keechie, her drum, her pipe and pouches of tobacco and pollen into it. Pulling the travois behind me, I made my way back to the Rock just as the sun was setting.

I left my boots outside the Sacred Ground and gathered Keechie into my arms. Then I carried her to the opening I had made. I placed her against the back wall, and as I sprinkled corn pollen over her, I called upon Puma Man and her ancestors to watch over her journey into the spirit world.

Outside of her resting-place, I loaded her pipe, lit it, and blew smoke to the four directions, then to the sky and the underworld below. I began beating her drum and chanting as we had done for her Pap and brother. I still didn't know the words, but I felt that the spirits recognized my intentions and knew the words anyway.

As I continued, I felt the presence of Puma Man descending upon me. I began playing louder and faster and the words began coming from my mouth. Keechie's voice seemed to join mine, singing with me as we had done so many times in the past.

Just then, a single ray of sunshine streaked up from the horizon and illuminated a cloud directly above me. In the cloud, I saw Keechie and the Puma Man looking down at me. I gave a final beat on the drum and held my arms towards them, until the cloud faded and darkness fell.

"Good-bye, my friend, Keechie—Spirit Singer of the Osochi Clan," I said to the dark sky.

After I placed the drum, pipe and pollen into the space with her, I filled the opening with rock. A small fire and the blanket from the travois kept me warm the rest of that night up there on the mountain with her. I just couldn't bear to leave her and return to this empty cave.

I stayed awake all night, just sitting there, remembering and re-living the things the two of us had shared since that first day at the spring. By sunrise most of my grief had been replaced by a feeling of appreciation for the very special gifts of her friendship, her knowledge, and her calm acceptance of whatever life dealt her.

The next week I returned to the reservation alone and told them of Keechie's death. They held a special ceremony for her at the Stomp Grounds. It looked as if the entire population of the reservation was there and they did the Ghost Dance in her honor.

I stayed there for three more years, teaching and learning more than I taught. Then I met your mom, we got married and had you, and now here we are, in Keechie's Cave.

We sat there in silence for several minutes until Alex said in a quiet voice, "I could hear you playing the drum, Daddy. While you were telling the story. I could hear it!"

"Me too, darling. Me too." I said, remembering Keechie's words from the day I had held old Bull Killer's spear.

"Didja hyer da drums, Brine? As long as dey is someone who kin hyer da drums, da People will nevva die."

References

Books

Angie Debo, *The Road to Disappearance: A History of the Creek Indians* (Norman: University of Oklahoma Press, 1941);

Michael D. Green, *The Creeks* (New York: Chelsea House, 1990);

Joel W. Martin, Sacred Revolt: *The Muskogee's Struggle for a New World* (Boston: Beacon Press, 1991).

Ballard, W. L. (1978). *The Yuchi Green Corn Ceremonial: Form and Meaning.* Los Angeles, CA: University of California American Indian Studies Center.

Cohen, Hennig and Coffin, Tristam. (1987). *The Folklore of American Holidays.* Detroit, MI: Book Tower.

Gerson, Mary-Joan. (1995). *People of Corn—A Mayan Story.* Boston, MA: Little, Brown and Company.

Rodanas, Kristina. (1991). *Dragonfly's Tale.* New York, NY: Clarion Books.

Rozakis, Laurie. (1993). *Celebrate! Holidays Around the World.* Santa Barbara, CA: The Learning Works.

Laubin, Reginald and Gladys—1977—*Indian Dances of North America.* Univ. of Oklahoma Press

Hawkins, Benjamin—1848—*A sketch of the Creek Country in the Years 1798 and 1799.* Georgia Historical Society Reprint

Pound, Merritt B.—1951—*Benjamin Hawkins—Indian Agent.* University of Georgia Press

Websites

The Muscogees or Creek Indians, from 1519 to 1893
http://homepages.rootsweb.com/~cmamcrk4/crkst1.html#anchor1280778

The Ghost Dance Among the Lakota
http://www.pbs.org/weta/thewest/resources/archives/eight/gddescrp.htm

GLOSSARY OF INDIAN WORDS
http://www.snyderweb.com/placenames/glossary.htm

CREEK LIFESTYLES & CUSTOMS (Legends, Medicine, Food and Festivals)
http://www.ryal.k12.ok.us/creek.html

Maize (The Maize Page) History, development,
http://maize.agron.iastate.edu/maizearticle.html

Who Were the Mysterious Yuchi Indians (The BAT CREEK STONE)
http://www.drwebman.com/euchee/yuchi/

An Introduction to the Creek Nation
http://ngeorgia.com/history/creek.html

The Creek Indians of Georgia
http://www.ourgeorgiahistory.com/indians/Creek/creek01.html

An Investigation of Muskogee Creek Indian Counting Words
http://www.ethnomath.org/resources/ISGEm/096.htm

Georgia's Indian Heritage
http://www.ourgeorgiahistory.com/history101/gahistory01.html

Encyclopedia of North American Indians—Creek (Muskogee)
http://college.hmco.com/history/readerscomp/naind/html/ na_009100_creek.htm

Ribbon Dance Notes (and other traditions)
http://www.freenet.tlh.fl.us/Museum/culture/RibbonDance- notes.htm

Wildflower and Herb Identification Tips
http://altnature.com/library/identifying.htm

Native American Legends
http://www.ucan-online.org/legends_list.asp?category=9

Printed in the United States
41806LVS00002B/349-420